Family
Lore

Also by Gerard Windsor

The Harlots Enter First
Memories of the Assassination Attempt
That Fierce Virgin

Family
Lore

Gerard Windsor

William Heinemann Australia

First published 1990 by
William Heinemann Australia
22 Salmon Street, Port Melbourne, Victoria 3207

Edited by Jackie Yowell
Designed by Lynn Twelftree
Typeset in 10pt Berkeley Oldstyle
by EMS (Evans Mason Services Pty Ltd), Melbourne
Printed in Australia by Australian Print Group

National Library of Australia
    cataloguing-in-publication data:

Windsor, Gerard, 1944-
    Family Lore.

ISBN 0 85561 389 0.

I. Title.

A823.3

For all my family

Acknowledgements

In slightly different versions, 'Virgins, Widows, and Penitents' appeared in *The Harlots Enter First* and 'My Father's Version of the Nurses' Story' in *Memories of the Assassination Attempt*. Other chapters appeared in the *Australian Literary Magazine*, the *Sydney Review*, the *Adelaide Review*, and the *Sydney Morning Herald*.

Contents

Starting
the
Family

I HAVE TWO grandparents, one male, one female. But they met only when she was five years past menopause. That was four years before I was born. My father's father and my mother's mother. To all practical effect I have no other grandparents.

Such are the facts. Yet the possibilities of moving on from them are endless, and I have to proceed with caution if I'm to retain the same degree of reliable simplicity.

Whom, for example, do I discuss first? My instinct is to do him, then her. But why? Suspect tradition? Male bias? So then should I do (or perhaps discuss or perhaps give an account of or perhaps . . .) her first? But then maybe I'm patronisingly letting the lady go first, or I'm allowing the organic spontaneity of my account to be disrupted by external orthodoxies? In any case, am I assuming too much of the account already, and hence distorting it, by labelling my grandfather male and my grandmother female? Certainly in her case that would have to be severely qualified. Besides, I'm assuming what are female, what are male characteristics. But then I am not as yet basing any step of any argument on the distinction. I can discuss their gender shadings entirely as a preamble. I can do that without actually proceeding anywhere.

'Would you ever get on with it, fulla,' says the old man.

He is more impatient than she. The force of his voice drags me back beside him. Maybe it rockets him forward here beside me. Whatever the spatial equation describing his movement, he won't allow me to treat him in any past tense. Whether the old lady makes the same demand, will make the same demand, I can't as yet tell. She may not even be an old lady, by the time I get back to her – or catch up with her. But the old man is incontrovertibly an old man; he wears glasses and a stern expression in the earliest surviving photograph of him.

In fact – although this wasn't one of the features I originally had in mind – in this first photograph, the bottom half of his body is covered not by trousers but by a crutchless piece of cloth, with not two openings at the bottom but only one. In other words, by what is basically a skirt. In essence, by a garment that does not call attention to the pressure of male thighs and the four-square sturdiness of legs, but envelops, so that it either advertises itself (hardly, in the present rather drab case), or it starts speculation about the mystery that it so comprehensively conceals.

Well . . . that might be a little excessive, for in the present instance my grandfather is actually wearing a soutane. I had set out to suggest that he had gained some female feature by choosing a skirt for his first public appearance. And maybe he has, in some ways. But the garment is not drawn in anywhere; hips, callipygous curves are hardly . . .

'What's the fulla sayin'?' shouts the old man.

It is not, admittedly, a very female voice. If I can just ignore it for a moment longer and stick with this photo. He is deaf, you see, and neither overhears nor is too put out by a slight hum of conversation near him. I concede that he is not very female in this photo. In fact he is sitting down on a step and the skirts of the soutane are rucked up over his knees in a most inelegant and quite unselfconscious manner. And plonked down between his legs, grasped firmly in his two hands held one above the other, and rearing up high over his head so that he has to peer around it, is this great, lit, brass candlestick. Now the soutane might be immediately identified as a clerical robe, and that would suggest asexuality. But such suggestion has to compete with the very eloquent burning pole. If you could only accept one message, you might be forced to make it the pretty powerful straightforward masculine one.

But there's the rest of the photograph and that would give anyone pause. My grandfather is sitting in the front centre of a mass of clergymen and acolytes, and the party is awash with camp frippery: birettas and lacy surplices and hands folded like dying swans round breviaries. Poking his way to the presiding position is a squat, ill-favoured master of proceedings.

'Cardinal Logue opened the cathedral,' says my grandfather.

Well, well, that makes sense. There he is, a good seven years after Simon Dedalus called him 'the tub of guts up in Armagh'. He hasn't done anything in the interval to make his appearance more edifying. Not an attractive lot, really. I'm not sure I care for a little boy like that getting mixed up with them.

'I've my back to the lot of them.'

So he has; he's further forward than anyone and he's got a firm grip on that candlestick of his. The peering face, the bunched-up legs, betray that he's looking out into the world, intent on the photographer's art and science. It hasn't even crossed his mind that the important thing about the moment might be himself, and his part in the momentous proceedings, and the face he's going to put on for . . . not posterity, but whoever it is that looks at group photos of childless men.

So maybe that's the one thing about my grandfather in that photo that finally impresses. Unlike the rest of the dignitaries and the functionaries on that occasion, he'll be regarded, he'll have children and grandchildren and so on, and they'll look at him all right. He doesn't need to strike a pose, put on a personality whose unambiguous force will impose itself on them, because they'll have all the time in the world and myriad other beams and motes of evidence to figure him out by. There's no way one studied, resolute image is going to paralyse them into unquestioning, filial awe. He won't be monochrome, he won't be univocal; he'll be a riot of contradictory pictures. So he has no thought for himself and he's looking out towards a bit of art and a bit of science, into the world to come, and he's probably never been photographed before, and he's just into secondary school, and the century still hasn't turned but is about to, and he's thinking maybe of surgery.

'My father has a colt to geld,' says my grandfather, 'and he's waiting to take me with him to help him. Will the fulla behind the shutter never get done? There's the most tremendous jet of blood out of a horse, and I marvel that the old man keeps himself so dry. But there's a drop of the blood gets here and there, and he likes to have me on hand.'

The old man – my grandfather that is, not his father – can talk. My father says the habit, a bad one, is, among those of his children who have it, inherited from the maternal side. He makes this point with some force any time he has sat through tea and a chat for an hour or two. He has not taken part, he points out, because he has throughout retained a book in his hand.

Where in hell are we? I think the point of departure was the assertion that my grandfather was perennially an old man. I could, maybe, find a circular path back to that. If that was the spot, I might as well cut straight across the country. And draw two modest, simple conclusions. The shot of my grandfather as an acolyte at the opening of the Sacred Heart church (not cathedral, as he would have it – understandably, being a smallish boy from a smallish town), Omagh, Country Tyrone, in 1898, probably does not say anything about his gender shadings (contrary to what I had thought on adducing that photograph). Nor, if one is to be soberly reasonable, does it allow too many deductions about the lineaments of the future. But it is not in my blood to restrict myself to sober reasonableness. Not that I imagine I want to say anything unreasonable, but I'll put my hand up for leaps of insight, bold hypotheses, daring speculations, passionate apologias, unbridled pilings-up of evidence, inspired enthusiasms, categorical denials – in brief, all the vigorousness you've a right to expect from that grandfather's grandson.

Having said that, I imagine I must make another qualification. For, if he was perennially an old man – and he was, because he was around as his sons' father for so long, came perilously close to outliving them, was present in the lives of umpteen people as *the* aged member of the species, and because, to so many of the children and younger ones in his circle, he may have had something of the bogey about him, forbidding, gruff, eccentric, speaking in no known foreign accent, pretty opaque behind his glasses and his tennis shade and his moustache – and surely all that's enough to validate the title of eternal old man. But, if he was that, he also had a striking number of traits that are commonly regarded as young. He worked, professionally. He had worked the day he fell over his radiator, broke some ribs, caught pneumonia, and died. He saw patients daily. Or, to be precise, patients came to see him, and he went through the routine of taking a history and examining them, but when he looked down their throats or into their ears or listened to their chests . . . 'I can't see or hear a demn thing. Blind and deaf. I shouldn't be taking their money. But I can't give it up.'

Whether such honesty is a mark of youth or age, who's to say? Other, apparently juvenile, activities might have a geriatric quality to them: in his late eighties he drove, he ran on the spot one hundred steps every night before bed. But it is surely a mark of youth that he asked questions, showed continuing interest in the living and the world, in addition to a fair quota of narrative and reflective talk on his own account.

So, yes, an old man all right, but not to have senescence predicated of him all the time. All that adds up, I think, to a moderate and accurate assessment of at least that issue. He was, he is, an old man. Is he female too? Significantly so? Dangerous ground of course – labelling characteristics as female and spotting them in him. I would probably have pointed to an exquisite gentleness with patients, a concern for the presentability and fashionableness of his domestic surroundings . . . See what I mean. Dangerous. Let's just say that all other factors considered – his greater age, his having travelled further, his bearing the same surname as myself – he has staked a right to priority of treatment.

It would be less fraught to pinpoint male characteristics in my grandmother. But I've said nothing at all about her so far, and it would be quite misleading to start with an account of her male side. She herself would never do justice – not in her speech she wouldn't – to her own more overtly feminine side, and there's no way I'm going to abet her conspiracy of self-denigration. And that's what it would be if I made deliberate play to bring out first of all the male quality of her. As it happens, these put-downs weren't too successful in convincing anyone. No matter how hard she tried, a certain realism kept re-establishing itself. Even the stoop, the increasing stoop which marked her progress through life, and was at its most typical as she went from the house towards the office – a grey-cardigan-covered, round-shouldered back, a small neat head, small bun on the nape of the neck – seemed the clerical worker's very own professional disability. But that was not the explanation she gave; she had the true philosopher's compulsion to seek first causes. 'It was carrying all those children,' she said. Being a linguistically sophisticated youth I took her as referring to her pregnancies. But this puzzled me because she'd only had two (in the three years, mind you, between virginity and widowhood). But I was being too clever by half for myself. 'Carry' in a straightforward mouth like my grandmother's could mean carry. She was the second child and eldest girl of ten children. She folded her hands under Claude's arms and lugged him a few paces on her belly when she was four. By the time she was six she had found the saddle on her hip for Frank, and by 1898 when she was ten, Kathleen was high in her arms on, if need be, permanent hold, and certainly no longer just a toy of which she was having a momentary go.

So my grandmother in her late twenties, unmarried and without children, is already marked by motherhood in the family group portrait, taken outside the back verandah – by the man she has said she will marry, and eventually does. Her head is on an angle and one shoulder is dropped lower than the other. Her sister Peg stands upright beside her, warning the camera, jaunty-bosomed, innocent of the cares of motherhood, impervious to its trauma. Forty years later Peg has my sister and myself to stay for a week. My mother must be having a baby. My sister and I fight most of the time. My aunt threatens me with her husband, my Uncle Frank, and enrols me in the town library. Thirty years later her daughter is incredulous that she invited us. 'She could hardly be bothered with her own children,' she says. No, the photo says as much; she is holding herself above and back from the younger members of the family seated in front; she is not bothered with, bothered by, children. It is another world she seeks. But my grandmother is already worn down by children. I would say that fact ensures her female rating. And it is not a matter of my subjective choice of an arguable quality, but the obvious presence of a condition universally acknowledged to be a peculiarly female hardship. Among other things.

'We were all busy, some of us in a hurry,' she says, 'and he was taking too long. Claude had to catch the train to Willow Tree. Peg was in a bad humour – Rita she was then, changed her name later, more fashionable. He fiddled with the cloth, and popped in and out, and tried to give us orders. Lovely equipment it all was, but oh so slow. He wasn't, what would you call it, such a manly, brisk sort of fellow as the boys were, Ralph and Claude, but oh he was such a nice man, very patient. A pity he's not in the picture there himself.'

My grandfather is determined to have his say on public appearances. Or at least his own father's say. ' "I'd keep as much of yourself hidden as possible," said my old man. He never took a fancy to my face. "I wouldn't go flourishing my dial, not if I were you I wouldn't." I took his advice. The day I could feel hair on my face coming on, I worked at it like a nigger, combing and watering and shaving the moustache into a bit of camouflage. I've kept it there ever since. A face is not so important to a man, you know. It's what he manages to get done that matters. A bit impersonal, but there you are. A man just gets on with it, shouldn't be worrying about putting his best face forward, or social diplomacy or any of the like. Straightforward. Doing what has to be done.'

'I shouldn't have married him really,' continues my grand-mother.

'It's why I got married,' he interrupts. 'Nothing to do with my face. I don't know that she ever looked at that. All the way out and all the way home from our walks on Sunday afternoons she had her eye on the ground. We were saying the rosary.'

'Father Forde warned me . . .' she admits.

'Gerry, come away from there. Leave her alone.'

Lord, what's my mother doing pushing in here? This is all premature. Marriages, my mother, and I haven't even settled the initial order of appearance. I admit I've simply assumed a start with my grandparents. Well, I've known them. Well then, I've seen them with my own eyes. A rather empiricist fallback? Well, let's say they were the first not mediated to me through others' eyes, words, tastes, and all the rest of it. I can get to on them without prejudice. It'll be just me and them. Except insofar as they refer to this or that relative or connection. Otherwise they'll be entirely my versions.

My father believes that the last few generations have seen an improvement in the family. Up to his generation, that is. Shutting out for the moment my father – who has no business here – I'd like to borrow his word 'improvement'. Improvement is my business. That's not to say I'll make these characters better, but then that's not to say I won't. The word can keep all the ambiguity my father doesn't mean for it. Why should I not touch up my grandmother here and there, heighten this feature, throw that one into the shade, pencil-brush the appendix scar or the inoculation mark out of sight – or bring them up into sharper, more heavily outlined focus? After all, I might like a scar. Its presence is not to be taken as a denigration. But then neither is its absence. Improving my grandmother has nothing to do with canonising her. The same, *mutatis mutandis*, for my grandfather.

'What about giving a fulla a name? The old lady too for that matter? She's not just your grandmother.'

It's what she is, primarily, to me. And it's my story.

'And the first thing you say about her is to do with her menopause. A young fulla like you shouldn't be talking that way.'

'Come off it. You're the one to talk. What are women to you except mothers, potential mothers, spiritual mothers – or rubbish?'

'What else could there be?'

'Well, take my grandmother, the old lady, for a start.'

'Yes, do that.'

Romance
as
a Beginning

AT SOME POINT I have to control the clamouring
voices and have my own say. You can listen only so long. There
comes a moment when you've got the point – or a point – and you
walk away and start acting. There's not much use in a jostling host
of ancestral bodies around you if you can't pick and choose and play
favourites and even then be selective in what you'll accept from
them. On the other hand it doesn't do to take your eye off what
you've passed over. Could be very dulling or a great mould for
complacency if you just grab what you like the look of or align
yourself only with the sort of company you think will flatter you.
With luck there'll be something for different ages, different moods.
   'The old lady! Have you anything to say about her?'
   'Yes. I like her style of romance.'
   'Oh, for the love of God, that's a predictable thing to say about a
woman now, isn't it? And what's that you accused me of?'
   'If you'd let me add the finer tonings . . .'

'A very gracious old lady, and a woman of business, you could have said.'

'But her style of romance was at the heart of it. It was qualified, considered, muted. Even at times dispassionate. I like that. Anyone can conjure up a voice from the past that is either all roses and sweet nothings or else embittered bleakness and contrition. But her style was more complex, more realistic. Far more useful for a latter-day descendant.

'Are you suggesting she was alone in that?'

'No, I'm not.'

He won't take it any further. He hasn't any of that blustering, panicky need to assert his own personality as the one most worthy of centre stage. But he has a right not to let me get away with over-neat genetic partitionings. 'I was on the staff of the Middlesex General Hospital. She was a nurse there. We used to walk out every Sunday, and as we walked back we said the rosary.'

He doesn't go much further with the recollection. When the year of his appointment finished he moved on. The story becomes obscure. I am the only one with any leaves of a text at all. And it's only my word that I've got that. The anti-romantic story is my line of business, and any version I present of my grandfather's courtship is likely to be written off as my perverse form of wishful thinking. What can I do but shrug my shoulders? The old man will ensure he has his own say.

'What appealed to you about her?'

'Oh, her walk and the Waterford brogue.'

I can't quite account for it, but already he is squeezing out my grandmother. I love her, admire her no less. I would rate her at least as colourful as him, but I take a step in her direction, and his shadow falls and I imagine I hear him calling, 'nothing there boy'. Of course this may be in fact the voice of his son, my father, who is much more likely to deflect attention away from what he sees as a garrulous, mercantile lot. The wife he has chosen from among them may have escaped the more suspect characteristics of the strain, but there's no telling what might recur in a later generation. He has every business to be guarding his own. He is not a believer in breeding, he has no acquaintance with terms like 'a better class of person', but his own people, he believes, are serious and con-tributory in the way that life calls for. He would be hurt – and it should not be written off as a self-inflicted wound – if they were not to continue that way.

'The family were hardly to my liking,' says my grandfather. 'All the comfortable old Carrolls up on the hill, living in filth, saying their prayers and abusing their neighbours.'

This interposition is smart-arsery to my father. He adopts a solemn, now-thank-we-all-our-God tone of voice, almost tearful. 'The family has come a long way in a short time.' He may be categorised as a tribal meliorist, but the stance's implications would trip him up. For however sincerely he looks for the progress of each new generation, he would have acute difficulty in acknowledging any as ultimately superior to his own.

His form of improvement represents a concentration, and concentration represents a narrowing of possibilities. My grandfather offers greater range. He is gallant, and offers all parties, if not their due, at least some hearing. So why does he tend to obscure the old lady?

'Try her out,' he says. 'She's had a hard life. And never had any sort of limelight.'

'Not that she wanted it.'

'Not that she wanted it. Give her her due. A story of heroism, if that's what you think.'

'Well . . .'

'Well what, fulla? A bit of feet-on-the-ground romance. Isn't that what you claim for her?'

True, she can be presented with a real upswing. One of six daughters, all lively and beautiful, and four sons, the children of a country storekeeper, an Irish migrant. And storekeeper does not mean merchant or retailer. Murrurundi never managed to find 2000 inhabitants. He went to Newcastle occasionally, to Sydney a few times, and once took his eldest daughter with him to Perth. She was engaged at the time; it was a kind of last fling for them both. He looked so young, she said. He never had a grey hair. The people there all thought he was my fiancé. Ahh, Dadda. They had their photo taken together again, he always in a chair, she leaning against the arm. None of the other daughters, none of the other children, ever managed it even once.

Or she can be part of a general rising note. 'Dadda only ever did one thing wrong in his life. He spent all his money on his children and never gave himself a trip back to Ireland.' But, as investments go, the money was judiciously placed. Those six girls had no inheritance. But they must have acquired something. One married a grazier, one a solicitor, and the other four all married doctors. Curiously, the four boys in comparison were failures. One died when he was twenty-four, the others grew old and no richer working that store or other men's stores. There is of course a shocking illogicality in my terms of comparison. I range the women's marriages against the men's business occupations. The girls acquired skills all right, nurses, a physiotherapist – but the fact is, it was their marriages not their professions which lifted them from the mere Irish into the gentrified middle classes. The Dooley girls they were, and it is striking that though they all married Catholics, good Catholics, they chose husbands with names that were not such a giveaway – Burfitt, Burns, Honner, Best, de Monchaux. Beautiful girls, talented girls, but hard-headed girls too. None of their brothers made a marriage that elevated them. The boys had dilatory, convivial, mildly dissipating habits. Horses and non-Catholic women overbore them. Ten children, and the name Dooley hardly survives. But the girls . . !

Still, that kind of merely social and material elevation is in fact a low form of romance. My grandmother is worth more than that. It hardly gives her a fair chance against the pressure of the old man. Sentiment gains tone from having her restraint to push against. 'I'll marry you,' she says, 'but not till you are through medicine.'

His future is not assured, and above all he is delicate. So in the meantime, being in no hurry, she has what she calls fun. This is not to be condescending or dismissive. It is her word, but she gives away nothing of what she means by it. To all appearances Dadda is the most important man to her. She is more than his darling, she is his assistant, almost his partner, certainly not merely the drudge. Their store is in its heyday. 'Fourteen men in the grocery alone in Dadda's time,' she boasts, but that is her time too. The fiancé coughing over his books and his cadavera and his patients 220 miles away, the fine edge of her celibacy goes into her choice of manchester and the scrupulousness of her account books and a no-nonsense charm with customers, and maybe into a little hero-worship and concern for – and even a tincture of romance – about her slightly older cousin Vince.

Now there's a demand for the rising note in that story. All through the long latter years of her engagement, Vince is first somewhere in England, and then somewhere in France. The massive underground mine explodes, and he clambers up onto Messines Ridge and goes forward into the storm of smoke and debris and he wins promotion to pips and a Military Medal. A year later he is still alive, and she writes to him just before her wedding. He gets the letter ten days after she is married. What does she say to the hero, that wide-eyed dispassionate woman, as she faces her marriage to the invalid? But two months later, when Vince's effects are gathered, all this overflow of her old life, her young life, is swept away.

All speculative, all speculative, and marginal in any case. I don't even need the old man to point it out. And far from letting her be elevated by the upswing, I'm possibly demeaning her. Any element of calf-mooning reduces her. Let's just say simply that Vince admired her, he virtually said so in his letters, and that her younger sisters all thought he was a lovely fellow. Which was not quite their attitude to the man she did marry. Marie, for one, was at boarding school at Moss Vale at the time, and during their honeymoon at Berrima they came over to see her. Marie was embarrassed and upset and ashamed to see her beautiful eldest sister with this pale thin man with a limp. They offered to take Marie out with them, but she said no. It was the shared, but individually appropriated, family attitude. When she insisted to Dadda that she was going ahead with it, he merely told her that if she was making her bed that way she'd have to lie on it. Dadda was a one for the cold eye in these matters. 'Dadda was engaged to a girl in Ireland. That's her there, a fine-looking woman. I said to him, "What happened, Dadda?" "Ah well," he said, "the letters went astray".'

Dadda's dispassion was long-standing, and impressive. Particularly in matters of the heart.

'There we were in the sitting room, Mumma as well as Dadda, and the children, still only Ralph and myself and Claude in arms. When in swept Mrs Farrell. Mr Farrell still owned the store. It was Farrell's General Store. But Dadda did all the work. Mr Farrell spent his time up at the Railway Hotel playing cards and drinking champagne. He was a gentleman. But Dadda made the money for him. And Mrs Farrell could spend it too. Yes, I don't know how many maids she had. Mind you she was a very capable woman, taught in the primary school. But she was fond of the drink too, and she'd a drop taken this night. In she swept, all done up in laces and furbelows, and the most beautiful chiffon parasol – I'll never forget · it, oh dear it was pretty – and there she was laying down the law, and being very domineering, and tapping her parasol on the table. And what was she doing but making love to Dadda, and Mumma was there and all, and her son Tom with her, and Dadda was taking it all very quietly you know, oh yes, and when she wasn't . . . you know . . . Dadda wasn't reciprocating in any way, she'd say "C'mon, Tom," and she'd go to the door, and then she'd come back again, and we were all so frightened of her you see, but Dadda was, oh so unmoved by it all.'

Dadda didn't interfere, much less inveigh or rage. When his eldest daughter voiced her own doubts to him, he advised her – no more than that – to talk to Father Forde. Father Forde had a solid reverence for the married state. When she spoke to him he praised the state in the person of her mother. Mumma, he told her, didn't know the meaning of the word 'sin'. But he doubted whether my grandmother would ever be given the chance to prove herself over such a long haul; the young man did not look a good prospect. But she was a woman of twenty-seven, she had been the companion and confidante to her father, the reserve mother to her siblings. This was her choice now. And she made it, not blindly by any means, not romantically. He was a lovely fellow; she had given her word; she had kept him waiting through those long medical years. And she was rewarded, enough, in a way. She didn't know anything at all about marriage, but he was very patient and very gentle with her. She said that much for him, more than once, and never said anything against him. They were married on 4 June and their daughter was born late in March the following year. 'Little Bubbie was just decent,' my grandmother said.

There's still too much of the rising note in that account, too much of the noble Roman maiden rising to her fate. It requires at least two qualifications. She never presented herself as duty's slave, and by culling the odd hints and presenting them all together I could be suggesting a firmness and a clarity of intention that was never there. She was fond of him and flattered by him, and the sense of obligation and responsibility and loyalty was just one barely distinguishable thread in all that feeling. Secondly, maybe, maybe there was just the faintest fear that if she didn't marry him she would marry no one. After all, the war had come and almost gone, and there were unnervingly fewer men to marry her generation. And she wasn't too sure that she measured up well in the competition, even with her own sisters. 'I was the plain Jane,' she said. Repeatedly. Enough to suggest she meant it. To a latter-day eye her case seems weak. From photographs at the ages of ten, fourteen, eighteen, twenty-five, twenty-seven, a reasonable judgement would be that she is at least on a par with her sisters. She is shorter than any of them, certainly, and maybe that loses points in her own book. Otherwise she has a distinctive appeal. I use the word deliberately. I hesitate about looking hard at my grandmother as a young woman – to say nothing of my mother – and asking would I – no, do I – find her attractive? Do I fancy her? But viewed thus my grandmother will assume proper status as a woman, and not be just a sentimental connection. After all, the very term 'grandmother' labours under an awful burden of connotations. Warm, snuggly, nurturing, generous, wise, patient, resourceful, a refuge, commonsensical, a buffer. More or less the litany of Loreto in fact, or at least its earth-mother, non-mystical, items. To a forty-year-old eye my grandmother has a mature attractiveness. Rarely without a smile, but always muted, and knowing. Her sisters smile too, but with the bright-eyed faces of children or the skittish self-consciousness of adolescents. Their poses are too much frozen; they have been barely restrained for an instant. They are exchanging giggles and remarks, part advice part teasing. They are determined to put their best face forward, but are equally determined not to be caught out in their vanity. Their mother, Mumma, sits in the middle, presiding all right, indomitable, but showing no pleasure in the event. Her eldest daughter has the serene smile of experience, not she. Fine-looking women, all of them. Not an unbalanced face, not a gross body or feature among them.

A disconcerting galaxy in fact for any man to approach. The sons stand with a democratic insolence about them. It's innocuous in the long run, but initially intimidating. And there is at least an aura of solidarity, of conspiracy amongst the daughters: their beauty, their number, their effervescent nimbleness – brave the man who approaches, and then tries to single one out. So the medical student my grandmother is to marry keeps his distance, remains separate from them, crouches behind his camera stand, covers himself with the black cloth. They, this twelve-person family ranged against him, chivvy him up. 'Hurry along, feller,' says Claude who has less than a year to live, 'I haven't all day.' He is catching the train, but only up the line to Willow Tree. The man in the black shawl trembles a little in his haste. Claude manages to look insouciant and debonair but he is impatient. The nervous photographer cannot afford to concentrate on him, and Claude begins to go out of focus. An arm lifts from the left shoulder of the black cloth and the hand is extended in an appeal for attention. My grandmother sees it pointing towards her. She cocks her head and relaxes into a smile that brims with affection yet is still wistful. While the others are part sideways on their chairs, and their teasings and complaints are still bouncing in the foreground, the featureless man behind the black mask pulls the cord.

So I chose death with my eyes open, I imagine her say, his death and the deaths of his generation. I placed my life in the shade of those deaths.

My grandfather's story has no such potential for the dying fall.

'I left the Middlesex without matters having come to a head. Maybe I had no thought that they should have come to a head. A few months later she resigned, and went home. Not to another job, just back to her family in Waterford. I made enquiries. Another man on the staff, a senior surgeon, had approached her. But the approach had been most unwelcome. Without her Sunday companion she felt exposed and vulnerable. She felt her position at the hospital was intolerable.'

But why abandon nursing, even if only temporarily? Why all the way home to Ireland? Was it a gamble to force his hand? As it happened, he did feel responsible; he imagined he must have compromised her. He was aware the charge could be made that he had first blocked any other traffic to the woman and had then merely trifled with her, and just at a period when she was entering her last-chance phase. After all she was thirty-three, four and a half years older than he. Whether she had intended it or not, he felt he had a duty towards her. Not that it was a stunning sacrifice. He had reached a professional stage when he was ready, he liked her, he respected her. So he asked, she accepted, and that was that.

The point about the old man's marriage is that the future still lies quite open. The deaths have not been anticipated, allowed for, and built around. It is the January of 1914; he is marrying but unwell. Six months later he is to take a sea voyage, by himself. He is ignorant whether it will recuperate him; he is unsure whether he should sail west or south; he is undecided whether he should simply travel or emigrate. There are rumours of war, in Ireland, but he is leaving the old hatreds behind. There is a child of his in the womb, and it is in another age that his mother has borne five children and he is the only one to be alive. It is in another country that the only sibling he has known, his elder sister, has died of typhus just as she had reached eighteen, or that the high colour on the cheeks of the first young woman the pubescent boy had had his heart race for has sunk to a cold ashen pallor. Not that he boards the *Osterley* as a naive utopian, but he is putting deep water between himself and the more openly ravening creatures of death. He is making his play for peace and a healthy life and an ebullient professional practice, and he has no idea or no thought now of how the shadow or the substance of death might find him out and dog him in such a new world.

'But the old lady,' he says, 'from the beginning was a woman of sorrow and acquainted with sorrow.'

Well . . . that's a bit fanciful.

In
the
Garden

WITH HIS PANAMA HAT on he sits in a cane chair. It is painted white, and of a deep sinous concavity so that he seems imprisoned in the bars of it. He holds a buff-covered medical journal, but it seems occupation for his hands rather than for his eyes or his mind. Every few seconds he gives it a couple of reflex jerks, partly to drive away the flies, partly to fan himself. Over his shirt he wears an alpaca coat, and although small drops of perspiration are gathering on his face, he makes no move to take off any clothes. His eyes follow the others around.

The woman kneels on the sugar bag beside the garden bed. She leans over the plants and digs around them firmly and energetically. Her fork slices briskly into the compact earth, and then rears its tips under the pressure of the heel of her wrist. The prongs come down again and tap, sometimes twice, sometimes three times, against the small up-turned clods. Periodically there is a break to the rhythm and the woman grubs in the opened soil and throws back onto the sugar bag beside her juvenile weeds that have never had a chance – nut grass and oxalis. At the end of her reach she leans back on her heels, then raises her haunches and steps back off the bag. Without standing upright, she drags the bag its own length again and returns to her weeding.

Under the eyes of her father, but nearer to her mother, the small child staggers about. She has her arms raised from the elbows for balance. She wears a white bonnet, and the left tape plunges under her chin, so that the ends of the ribbon can flutter from a flamboyant bow below her right ear. Her feet are bare on the lawn but she is not yet old enough to anticipate and fear the vulnerability of unprotected skin. She lurches and bounces to the edge of the lawn. Her mother does not look up, but she stretches out her free hand. It wills stability and balance for the child. It doesn't even try to be a physical preventative.

The father's hands grip the side of his chair and he poises himself. The bonnet and the ribbon hide the child's face from him. He cannot see whether she is fearful or intrepid or unconcerned. He sees only a tiny, swaying figure and outstretched arms.

The arms reach towards a daisy bush. The flowers lean towards the child across the guttering of the garden bed. Her fingers close around the nearest bloom. She tugs, and a segment of white-bladed petals comes away in her hand. She opens her fingers and looks at the disjoined, barely recognisable components of a flower. She bangs her hands together and flushes them away. She leans out again, fastens on a stem behind the nearest bloom, and tugs. The whole bush leans towards her and shudders.

'Leave the flowers alone,' calls her mother sharply.

The child jerks at the stem.

'Come here,' says the mother, and she swings back on her haunches, trails the fork on the ground in a ready position, and looks sternly at the child.

The child does not release the stem, but she swings her body from side to side in teasing defiance.

'Leave the flower alone,' repeats the mother.

The man waves his journal weakly. 'Oh come on,' he says, 'let her be. There'll always be plenty of daisies.'

The woman looks over to him. As she turns, her expression is still annoyed at the interference. Then she meets his eyes as he settles back into the long deep welcome of the chair. She hesitates a moment, then turns away, biting her lip, and plunges her fork hard through the surface of the rich soil.

'You've got it wrong again,' says my mother. 'It was Daddy who told me not to pick them.'

Virgins, Widows, and Penitents

THE OLD DOCTOR finishes the last spoonful of his baked custard, pushes his plate away brusquely, and wipes his moustache with his serviette. 'Thank you, dear, thank you, dear,' he says to the housekeeper opposite him. He rises, goes into the bathroom and expectorates, then clumps his way, splay-footed, into the lounge-room and sinks into his easy-chair. He looks out over the colourless desert of his night and steels himself for the passage. He lights a cigarette, smokes it evenly, with satisfaction but without greed, and stares high at the opposite wall, blankly amongst photos of his dead wife and family brides. It is two hours till the woman brings him tea, and joins him, on request. It is a gesture; normally other people are too much trouble for him now. Yet sometimes he wonders whether he doesn't actually fret for a body going through its normal paces more or less beside him. Even with the woman the notion assails him that the correct thing to do would be to reach out and caress her hand or tap her lightly on the shoulder. Sometimes. At appropriate times. Whenever that is. But the thought sounds suspicious. And then only at times can it in any case be called a temptation. At other moments quite the opposite. He cannot yet deliver his summing-up on women. Or perhaps on himself faced with the ebb and flow of their pull on him. He lifts the peg-board from beside his chair, adjusts the wad of unruled paper, and begins to write generously across it with a blue felt pen.

My personal wisdom is meagre. That however is not a remarkably humble claim. I stand by it, but eighty-seven years, more or less, of sermon attendance have convinced me that wisdom anywhere tends to be thin. I was in fact three when I was judged fit to attend Mass weekly. I have heard little over the subsequent years that I could say has struck me. The clergy have been parsimonious with truly instructive thoughts. Their line of work is wisdom, but in all charity I cannot give a high rating to their professional standards. Unless they have something to offer I feel they should be silent. Of course there is no profundity in that, but the depressing fact is that very few human beings believe they have no right to preach. Give some of them a black suit and a collar and there's no calling them back. But in a lifetime of wheedling, cajoling, admonishing and fulminating they hand out very little that's well-baked and nutritious. I do say this more in sorrow than in anger. Partly out of chagrin at my loss I admit; why should I have heard some five thousand two hundred and twenty-four sermons, to date, and have carried away so little spiritual baggage? Why should I have lost some one thousand seven hundred and forty hours, seventy-two and a half days of my life with virtually nothing to quicken my soul? When I succumb, as I've a weakness for doing, to rash judgement, I consider that the priests will have much to answer for. They've demanded so much yet given so little.

There's no point, as well as no justice, in condemning. Rather, I have been asking myself – and naturally enough too at my time of life – whether sermons are possible without preaching. Or perhaps preaching without sermonising? Words fail me, but the meaning is obvious. Personally I have always been most affected – I realise that is not identical with most enlightened, but enlightenment if it comes at all comes through affection – I have been most affected by the saints. I mean not so much the elite group, as all those here who are about to from their labours rest, and go marching in, and the rest of it. The living more or less. Those I have encountered at close quarters. So I should like to try my hand at a panegyric. The preacher need not be too prominent. Besides, the clergy's monopoly of the medium has always made me particularly envious.

Thy beauty now is all for the kings delight. (Common of Virgins). This is a most embarrassing text. It was chosen, I imagine, some one thousand years ago at least. He was a bold sort of lad that dug it out and got it through. It must all have been the most extreme piece of luck. For the life of me I can't see it being passed by any of the churchmen I know. And to be honest with you I wouldn't blame them. Metaphors for divine love are all very well, but to pay honour to a virgin by the public announcement that her beauty now is all for the king's delight, strikes me as really a gross piece of irony. But if you've no sense of irony and even less sense of sexual matters, you might find it wholly appropriate. There are such people and at least once I have found nothing ridiculous about them. About her to be precise.

When the Japanese took over the islands, a convent of Carmelite nuns was evacuated south to Brisbane and set up out at Auchenflower. Australians, Frenchwomen, others too I imagine. Not long after they arrived I was called out to see one old nun, the oldest there I believe, something over eighty. She was a Frenchwoman, from the same area and much the same age as Thérèse of the Child Jesus, though of course Thérèse was dead over fifty years by then. Never an especial object of my devotion I must admit. Whether the two had ever met or lived together, I don't know. I rang the bell as usual, the extern nun came and let me in, then bobbed ahead of me along the dark panelled corridor, ringing her tocsin to warn the intern nuns to avoid my sight. The Reverend Mother informed me about the patient: never had a day's illness in her life, but the fear of war and the sudden uprooting after fifty-odd years in the one building had proved too much. Reverend Mother didn't specify the illness – not that it was her business.

War and transplantation had nothing to do with the ailment as it turned out. I followed Reverend Mother to the old Frenchwoman's cell. She knocked, opened the door without waiting for an answer, spoke a few words that I missed, then withdrew, motioned me in and shut the door. Diagnosis was immediate. The patient stood back against the opposite wall, her hands clasped under her scapular and her head bent forward so that her eyes would not have taken in even my feet. The only part of her body exposed was the shadowed oval of her face, framed by her wimp. But the cell was noisome, nothing less. Reverend Mother, I am sure, had called me in on the strength of nothing more than that. I had come across enough similar cases – old biddies living alone or, a couple of times, with an equally aged brother too far gone in manners or prudery or necrosis of the senses to notice. Prolapses of the uterus. A degree of incontinence is only one of the manifestations. Female tissue of that area is of course rich in secretions; they are best kept internal.

I told the old nun I would have to examine her, and asked her to take off what was necessary and lie down under the coverlet on her bed while I waited just outside. She didn't move, in fact gave no sign that she'd even heard. Imagining she was deaf I repeated the instruction more loudly but she still gave no sign at all of having heard. Then I remembered she was French and probably, over a lifetime of silence, would never have had occasion to learn English. I went to take her by the elbow and get her to lie down on the bed, but her arm tightened and she moved back right against the wall. I had to be firm and make myself understood – it shouldn't have been hard; she must have known why I was there. But the instant I made to grasp her firmly by the arm she wrenched herself away, and her arms flew up, crossed over her bosom in the manner in which the artists always portray Agnes, Cecilia and the rest of those girl martyrs. I pulled at her, but those crossed arms were immovable. For an ailing woman in her eighties the strength was unnatural, and she made it all the worse by throwing up her head, looking high on the wall above me and beginning to scream. Not just a shriek, but words, the same phrase over and over again. I've no French: I couldn't understand her.

I stood back and left her alone. But she didn't let up. Just hugged herself and screamed and screamed with a passion and grief that I now, looking back, find awesome. At the time I was simply annoyed, and, I suppose, a little self-concerned. I went straight out of the cell, and tackled the Reverend Mother who was standing a few yards along the corridor in the usual posture of piety. I was offensively aggressive. 'What's the woman saying?'

She sounded apologetic as she articulated, in the whisper that was probably the only voice she'd used for the last forty years, '*Il m'a vu*, Doctor. He has seen me,' she explained.

'Well I damn well haven't,' I came back at her. 'Bloody waste of time. I don't expect any patient to behave like that, least of all you people.' And I started ahead of her down the corridor. She began to ring her tocsin and with a shade more urgency than on my arrival.

Four days later she rang me. 'Sister will see you, Doctor, if you could be so kind as to come out again.' When I arrived just before their dinner, the Reverend Mother said, 'I've had a word with Sister. I think she understands everything now.'

And of course there was no trouble. She was the most charming and gracious old lady. By then I was humbled a bit myself and was conscious of trying to make it as easy for her as possible. Over the intervening days that act of hers had taken something of a hold on me. It'd be ridiculous of me to get too melodramatic about it all; I don't want to do that, but I began to get a sense of the passion behind that scream, and I admit that with time it echoes even more inside me. 'He has seen me.' Of course I hadn't, at that time. But the sense of violation was so overwhelming that the future came at her in a rush and blotted out the present. All those years, seventy-odd of them, barely ever spoken to a man, except I suppose her father and various anonymous priests through the confessional grille. They were the full extent of her sexual dealings, the bride of Christ through and through. And then suddenly, when she had almost made it, some rough foreigner of a fellow breaks in and tries to make her lie down and submit to him – and what would be the difference to her now between that sort of examination and the gross activity she had forsworn and so decisively risen above? She must have wondered where her God was, maybe even wondered what sort of a sick, cruel lad he was at all.

It jolts me even now, a bit. 'He has seen me.' I was he, representative man I suppose. Man finally had seen her, got at her, and it makes me feel a terrible awful inadequate blunderer. I hope it was the worst of what she meant, for I sometimes imagine she meant the devil more than man, or at least that she made no distinction between the two. To this day I am sure I did nothing at all reprehensible, but to her I was the devil himself; and she was the most charming old lady and in the end, by an exertion of obedience

I don't like to think of, she submitted herself to me.

In the corridor beyond the door the housekeeper passes and repasses. The old man takes no notice of the momentary shadows. He begins on a new page.

Honour widows that are widows indeed. (1 Timothy 5:3). I'd have thought it was a straightforward, yea or nay matter, like virgins or the dead. Either you are or you aren't. But on reflection I concede it's a title that you've got to earn. Widows, widowers, all of us. Twenty years ago I thought I'd qualified automatically, but I don't know now whether I really rank. Further on in the book the apostle says a widow has to be desolate. Now that's a strong word, and hard as I've found it to be alone, and vehemently as I would urge seventy as the age at which a man really needs to marry, I still would feel a wee bit of a Pharisee, a wee bit of a fraud, if I told you I was desolate. I've no idea how many fit the bill, but I've seen one case that does, and by that standard I certainly don't.

I arrived in the hospital one morning just after eight. It must have been September or thereabouts; the early morning Brisbane warmth was getting into its stride again. The matron, not a woman for leisure at all, was waiting about the desk for me. 'We've an urgent, Doctor,' she said. 'Up in the convent.' The second phrase came as we swung off into the corridor, and she said no more till we were upstairs and on the walkway leading across to the nuns' own quarters. And all she did then was mention the nun's name. I was surprised, though only as much as professional experience allowed me; the woman mentioned was young enough still, had always looked healthy enough, and I'd no recollection of her having been seriously ill. At the door of the patient's room the Matron took a key from somewhere in the white folds of her habit. I frowned; sick rooms are never locked. I felt a spurt of irritated censoriousness against her. I couldn't help it, but I shouldn't have. I had always had the utmost professional respect for the woman – and I liked her too, I should add, in case the assessment sounds begrudging. But I couldn't help jumping to condemn her. The trait's not unusual but it's depressing to dwell on for all that.

At all events, as I entered the room, annoyance was still distracting me, when I should really have been warned by the locked door to expect something unusual. As it was I was still aware of the Matron locking the door behind us as I approached the bed. Then, at least, my professional machinery showed its condition and allowed me to process a rush of reactions quite instantaneously. For the nun in the bed had ceased being a patient, and was emphatically dead. I went through the routine of pulse and forehead, although the Matron needed that act even less than I did. There was nothing remarkable about the dead nun; at the most her body was slightly clenched. She wore all her regulation issue, cap and modest cotton nightdress, and her arms lay by her sides under the bedclothes. I looked up at the Matron. She said, 'I'd be glad if you'd write us the death certificate and look after the autopsy,' and her eyes held mine just enough to draw them across the bedside table. On it lay a syringe and several ampoules, their necks broken off. I could not at the distance read their labels.

Naturally I did what was required. On several previous occasions where the discretion of a good Catholic practitioner was needed I had been involved. I officially confirmed the death then and there so that the Matron was free to arrange the corpse. I didn't ask whether it had been previously tampered with. She did little more than fold the hands across the chest in the approved manner and, after a noticeably long search for the objects, she entwined the dead nun's rosary and metal crucifix around her fingers. I didn't like to question the appropriateness of this gesture although the irony of it was brought home to me forcefully later on.

Briefly, the subsequent history of this case was as follows. The nun had died from a solid, but economical injection of morphine; she was a fine nurse and knew her pharmacology; she did not believe in waste. My direct knowledge of the woman was slight, and it was the business of her religious superiors, not me, to go into the question of motivation. I don't know what happened about the funeral; I hardly made any effort to gather details, before or after. This was in the days when suicides were not allowed burial in consecrated ground. I imagine, in fact hope, that the nuns found for their sister a way round that rule. Probably along the lines of avoiding scandal in the faithful. Just like the old rule about mortal sin and communion: no one is obliged, given certain circumstances, to shun going to communion and thereby betray that he or she is in mortal sin. One of the Church's moments of eminent good

29

sense, that. And I imagine the convent would have a similar feeling for its own. But the girl's – woman's – death had its full impact on me when I discovered, in the course of my autopsy, that she was three months pregnant. The Matron was assisting me, no one else was present, and the moment I realised the cadaver's condition I passed on with as much affected professional equilibrium as I could muster to the next item on the routine agenda. I said nothing to the Matron, nor she to me. She may have missed it, but to this day I can't be sure. Given the woman's shrewdness and medical knowledge, I suppose it's wishful thinking to hope that she did.

Whatever of that it was the existence of the foetus that let me see into the desolation of that one-time bride of Christ. I cannot imagine a more complete widowhood than that. I've no idea what led her into the arms of some altogether more human male, but patently there was something wrong with the original marriage. She'd lost that husband somewhere, and just moved further away from him, down towards the centre of the Chinese boxes. There can't even have been a shadow of him by the time she pulled the last five walls down on herself, and it was then that she discovered that she had the child with her. Yet, she was absolutely alone, in a way that could release, even in someone who had never formed any bond at all, the most chilling desolation.

The housekeeper puts down the coffee table, then returns with the tea tray. The old man watches her with a dull dispassion as she pours his milk, his tea, adds his sugar and stirs it. When she hands it to him he lays it on the armrest, and lights a second cigarette. When he has drawn his first puff he looks at the food on the tray and gestures towards it with the cigarette, saying, 'What's that?'

She lifts the plate to him. 'Shortbread. It's nice and fresh.'

'Hey?' he asks. 'Speak up, woman.'

'Fresh shortbread,' she repeats.

'No thanks,' he says and waves it away.

They sit and drink in silence. He stares at the brides and the dead on the far wall and shoots out his smoke towards them. The woman looks towards her knees and several times brushes and smooths down her lap. Once, he makes an effort and says, 'Have you enough for the weekend?' 'Plenty, plenty,' she shouts mildly. Otherwise he is silent, distracted by the saints. When he has finished both cigarette and tea, the woman lifts his cup and saucer onto the tray, removes them, replaces the coffee table and disappears. As he reaches to pick up his board the old man notes her absence. He holds his bent pose an instant and murmurs, 'Thank you, dear, thank you.' But for a moment, before he starts on the clean sheet of paper, he gazes through it, distractedly.

Blessed are the undefiled in the way. (Mass of St Mary Magdalen, Penitent). This, to my encouragement but still to my bewilderment, is how the fellows responsible choose to sing the praises of a penitent. I would never have imagined myself a Platonist, but such surprising wisdom must have an existence of its own quite apart from any mind I have encountered. Not the most idolatrous devotee of paradox would label as *undefiled* what's always been thought of as *soiled* goods. Repentance may well be a saving grace, but it hardly seems to warrant such generosity.

God knows how sin affects the soul. Chemical reactions are complicated enough; moral corrosion mocks any analysis. Set the process in reverse, try the catalyst of repentance, and the result must be profoundly incalculable. The psalm for the Penitent comments, in its wisdom, *I have seen an end of all perfection: thy commandment is exceedingly broad.* Make of that what you can. But it's wise, I'd bet on that. The language itself is too fine to allow any admixture of rubbish. But it sounds as though the penitent might be the daddy of them all. And I'm mystified by this notion of latitude; an infinity of ways of making good, I imagine.

I could never put a finger to all the skeins by which we lower ourselves down to vice any more than those by which we haul ourselves up. I couldn't even mark the turning point of the pulley.

Some years ago I was in my rooms when four of the hospital nuns called in to see me. It was Christmas time; they had been doing their shopping and merely called because they knew I'd be going over to the hospital in the afternoon. They'd catch their breath in the rooms, they said, and then we could all go back to work together. I knew all of them, but one not much more than by sight and by name. She was a stout girl about forty, from somewhere up near Innisfail. She worked in the Children's. We had a bite to eat, or at least I did; somehow nuns still tend to be unobtrusive at such activities.

We found a cab at the rank on the corner of the Terrace. The women put me in the back, seemed to think my age warranted it. Two of them in with me, two in the front. The lady I didn't know opened the front door and got straight in; it was the others insisting on my welfare or what-have-you. Yet the comparative stranger was by far the youngest, and the discourtesy was all the starker contrast. To tell you the truth I couldn't swear I consciously noticed this at the time, but it rose up and fitted a pattern just a few minutes later. Heaven knows what the conversation was as we swung around and accelerated up the Terrace – family, other nuns, gallantries and teasing of one kind or another.

You don't see much from the middle of the back seat of a taxi, not with five other people in it. You keep your eyes to the front and rest your attention on things other than the sights. So I don't know how long it took for me to become aware of the central object of my field of vision – the head and shoulders of the Innisfail woman. But they were shaking, or rather convulsing, shivering, and then I heard her breath too, distinctly louder than normal, a variety of gasping, but uneven and staccato as though some effort were being made to control it. It was a normal December midday, there was no airconditioning in the cab, the woman had not been in this condition as late as our standing together on the footpath. My hand reached out, as an instinctive gesture to the driver, the natural, split-second forerunner of a call for him to pull over because I thought the poor woman was having a fit. What stopped me I don't know. But I didn't call. I just let my hand rest on the back of the seat, and, as we were swinging left away from the Normanby turn-off, I hope the gesture looked natural enough. I'm not a man of the world – for good or ill. Some of those women in the cab with me had much more claim to the title, and any insight I had must have come to them far sooner and with much greater clarity. I'm not sure that I had ever actually seen a woman in that condition. The admission perhaps damages me. Perhaps it exalts me. I've no idea and in any case it's not relevant. Neither had the other nuns ever seen it, I imagined, but I'd lay odds they knew exactly what was going on. My evidence for that was circumstantial but foolproof; all three of them redoubled the pace and the volume of their conversation. The woman next to the driver stayed in much the same condition until we all got out; she didn't seem in the least embarrassed when she said goodbye to me and went inside.

One of the others – I'd prefer not to name her – stayed behind. We knew one another well enough. 'It happens every time,' she said. 'She always makes sure she sits next to the driver. We all notice it, but I suppose we don't like to admit it to one another. I'm sure she's no idea what she's doing.'

I felt in no position to comment on that. I believed it. Riding, chaperoned, in a cab is certainly an unlikely occasion of sin. So I simply said, 'You can hardly confine her. But you can't have a performance like that taxiing round the town. One of you should have a word to her. It's a woman's problem.'

No, I wasn't buying out of it. I'd dealt with the husbands of too many women with that imbalance, and I knew it was no man's business to admonish or even advise a woman that nature had afflicted with such a condition. For it to be a nun made it no worse. In fact I imagine it was what they call a dispensation of providence: God saved some poor fellow from her. And these husbands are pitiable fellows too; no manhood left at all, the way they are forced to come to me for advice, any magic word that might get them a moment's peace. But that's neither here nor there. The point is this. From that day to this, that nun, the Innisfail woman, has never, to the best of my knowledge, taken the front seat in a cab. On the few occasions I've been present she's been more discourteous than ever on getting in. Into the back. But I have seen that it's almost a terror about being left to take the front seat. She cannot afford womanly modesty and reticence; they are luxuries that the healthy and unthreatened can indulge. But she has a devil to torment her and a justifiable savagery has entered her soul. I only know that she was never given any order, at least not by any human superior. It was her own war entirely and the difficulty of it must be appalling. Whether and where she believes sin enters it, I've no idea. But there is a threat to her soul for which she can allow no tolerance. Call her simple, call her neurotic, call her the washed-out victim of scruple and authority – and I'd have no vehemence in denying any of the epithets – but I can't get past the fact that she has set her hand to the plough and will, at any cost, subdue the stubborn earth, dust, clay, that is herself. Beside a cause like that, all other devotions and crusades have a quality of histrionic self-indulgence; whereas constant self-evulsion from the front seat of a cab sounds more the stuff of farce than of heroism, and it's that very quality that assures the purity of her zeal.

I'm going beyond my own guidelines: I'm pontificating. While the light, if any, is supposed to be on the woman. And the point is that the stout lass from Innisfail, with the degrading affliction and the discourteous manner, is storming the kingdom of heaven.

The old man drops his pen and hoists himself up by the arms of his chair. He stands some seconds to let the blood circulate, breathes deeply ten times, runs the same number of paces on the spot, then strides across the room and picks up a box of chocolates from the polished top of the dead television. He slides the lid off and holds back the enveloping folds of paper to look at the selection. He plucks out four empty mahogany-brown paper cups and screws them up in his pocket. He rearranges the selection so that the surviving chocolates are spread evenly across the cardboard surface, the hard centres grouped at one end, the soft at the other. Then, holding the box far out in front of him and intent on the stability of its contents, he moves out through the breakfast room and the kitchen. At the opening into the verandah alcove that is his own bedroom, and the annexe to the housekeeper's room, he pauses and calls through.

'Hello there, dear?' he says. Then he passes straight through into her room.

'What is it, Doctor?' she answers, but the words are indistinct, for her teeth are already in the glass.

'Would you have a chocolate for me, dear?' he asks her.

Neither of them look at one another.

'I couldn't . . . deal with it properly, at the moment.'

'They're very soft, down the end. Take one of those now.' He stabs a finger towards the selection.

'It's a bit late to be eating.' But she gives a quick laugh, part pleasure part tolerance.

'I'd have been here earlier, dear, if I'd had my wits about me. I'll come earlier in the future. But you'd still be able for a chocolate now, surely?'

'It's terrible the sweet tooth I've got,' she concedes. 'They're no good for me, I know.'

'One cigarette at my age does no harm to the body, but there's a lot to be said for its good to the soul. Have a chocolate for me, dear.' There is a pause. She repeats her quick laugh. 'You choose one for me, Doctor.'

His fingers hover above the box, unable to make any decisive distinction. They plunge in blindly, raise a chocolate and thrust it towards her.

Again she laughs and lets it suffice for her thanks.

He goes out and stands in the kitchen, trembling from the act, staring through the half-open window on the Tower Mill Motel. It is, they tell him, a favourite first night stopover for honeymooning couples. It looks an uneven unfinished patchwork of light and darkness. As he gazes, his nerves still open, he clearly beholds the young things rising in continuous procession through the lights and shadows, through the ecstasy and fading of their passion, up towards the dome of the pointing tower. And he sees himself with them. And the tower is a ladder set up on the earth, reaching into the heavens, and he sees the couples all, angels, ascending and descending upon it.

Continuing
the
Story

'*I HAVE SEEN* what people are capable of,' says my
grandfather. 'You need to know this. The most unlikely characters
have the demons set up house in them. In your profession, of
course, it's best you understand this. But – and this is not properly
appreciated – the profession itself has got as bad as anything you'll
ever see elsewhere.'

He says this to me in the dining room of Lennon's Hotel. He has
taken me to dinner there, in the middle of the day. He has told me
exotic stories: I had no idea my own family, the sharers in mere
blood and birthdays and seasonal gatherings, could have had a part
in such drama. Most of the time I keep my head down, and slice and
then re-slice my chicken maryland, as exotic a dish as the era can
offer – or maybe as I can associate with myself. There are limits to
what I can take in and digest. Potato croquettes and diced marrow
are not my everyday fare. I take them neither whole nor by
themselves. I add a sliver of one to a segment of the other, and the

bent of my eyes and the surface of my attention are concentrated on the operation.

'Watch Gerry,' says my mother, 'see how he holds his knife and fork, and cuts things up properly.' The younger children turn their heads and look, and the youngest among them try to readjust their grip. I wave my knife down the table towards my mother in lordly acknowledgment of her compliment.

Table manners shield me from my forbidding grandfather. He has a moustache, and glasses he never takes off. He grew up in a foreign country, and believes that boys are best brought up on boxing and swimming. I prefer my mother's mother who is kindly and protective and washes her hair in front of us on the back lawn. But the old man is my father's father, and there is no one older. Once he had an older wife who lay in a coma for years. He would visit her for hours every day, and her lips were the only things about her that ever moved, just a small twitching. He kissed her a lot on those lips, and said the twitch was her giving him a kiss, and he liked to see all his grandchildren lean over or get lifted up onto the bed and kiss her on the lips too.

'You'll find everything among your own people,' he says, 'every kind of sickness and crime that you'll find in the rest of the world. Alcoholism, suicide, pregnancy, murder, all the rest of it.' He is not talking about the literary world. I am going to be a priest, and he is making sure my eyes are open.

'I suppose there would be,' I say, but only because it would never occur to me to contradict him. He compels no belief that such exotic mayhem could ever be let loose in the pious world that I already know, almost at first hand.

'Take the old man's stories with a hefty pinch of salt,' says my father. 'Ninety per cent imagination, and maybe the other two per cent fact.'

'Your father would never believe these stories,' continues the old man, unprompted. 'Refused to believe it possible of priests and nuns. Until he ran into a case of his own.'

'Gerry,' they all say now, 'you have no right to be telling these sorts of stories, much less attributing them to the old man. And certainly not when you're really just making them up.'

The truth is that their stories would never occur to me. I would like to spin spectacular stories. And spin them out of my guts. All the complexity and marvel that the world is capable of, but the muscles of the heart, the lining of the bowel laid bare, quivering so recognisably that it hurts to look, but look you must. But no softening either of the cerebral edge, nor anything flabby or extraneous on the clean limbs of prose. All those dissociated qualities – feeling and control, personalised trauma and cold dispassion – all of them making up the plaited muscle of the corpus.

'I wasn't contacted till there'd already been several deaths,' relates my grandfather. 'A third woman got sick, and they realised she had all the symptoms of the previous two, so the Reverend Mother contacted me. This was down in Beaudesert, you see, so the woman hadn't wanted to trouble me earlier, because of the distance. It came out later there'd already been a number of strange things going on. Nothing to do with a doctor, it seemed, so it never got to my ears. It was a school they've got there, the parish school, and it appeared they'd had vandals breaking in. Obscenities written all over the blackboard – terrible things, quite foul. Luckily they came across them before the children arrived. The police were called in, but they didn't find anything. Nothing damaged as far as they could see, doors, windows, locks.'

My grandfather has a distinctive way of telling stories. He tells them readily, he likes repeating them, but he could not be classified as a raconteur. He does not have the exuberant relish about him. He is leisured and accretory. The cast of his head and the measure of his voice define him: the telling of each story is, in a manner, a regretful affair. These things have happened, it is the way the world is, and each particle of the story must be brought forward, openly and in its good time, so that it can be acknowledged and left exposed as a reminder. My grandfather is not doleful: I have never seen him looking lugubrious; his stories are never anything as crude as jeremiads, his narrative is never ponderous. But behind even a joke he is recounting you can hear the sigh of a man who spends his days watching the most ingenious of systems break down, and then does what he can to set going some alternative version. He excises, or drains off, the malignant matter, chooses the new points of conjunction, sutures the wound, so that there is again a passable subject for filtering, for absorbing, for decoding. He mixes, not some elaborate chemical formula, but a domestic balm of milk and whisky. He funnels it in and the raw system begins to process again.

'Crude,' says my grandfather, 'but you make do with what you've got. You give the lad life any way you can.'

Vitalist, organicist, I tell myself.

'What are you saying?' says my father. It is less a question to me than a jab of irritation. I'm not someone he takes any natural pleasure in. He finds nothing of himself echoing there. All the talk he hears is mocking or simply to no purpose. These are the objectionable, corrosive qualities of his wife's family. Frustration and anger are never far below his surface. They interfere with his listening.

'Some of these people you write about and review,' he says – and he is attempting to shift the complaint to an impersonal level – 'well, they've missed the whole point of writing. It's no use doing it unless you're going to be understood. How can you influence people and get things done if you're not going to make your message clear to them in the first place. Everyone can read Dickens. He wouldn't have reformed the poorhouses and sweated child labour and schools like Dotheboys Hall if he hadn't been clear in what he was saying.'

I don't argue with my father, but I don't think his position is contemptible. He has never heard of Auden and poetry making nothing happen, but even if he had he would have no time for the claim. I could try a few suggestions on the varied uses of literature, or even of writing. But it would be pointless and patronising to attempt to broaden my father's horizons. He might keep quiet and adopt a pose of listening, but I would be able to see the rock rolled firmly into place before any aperture in the mind, and he would wait until the fruitless attacks had spent themselves and then he would emerge, unscathed, and assert the unfractured validity of his position. I have neither the heart nor the enthusiasm for the dribbling advances. I hold no contrary view of the nature of literature with even a blush of that vehemence.

'There you are,' says my father, 'that sort of talk. Words, words.' He hunches forward and tenses as though pained by the wounds in his belly and his groin. 'You know, I think your own sister thinks your writing is bullshit. Not that she used that word.'

A false move. I feel for him. I'd be kicking myself later if I'd let that slip out. It's not a matter of my rising above anything, nor of simply being priggish. I feel inviolable, and the gesture, the strategy, catch my attention more than the content of the charge. It's the anger in him demanding to go free. He shouldn't betray people like that: it's not quite ethical. The camouflage is so transparent: on this matter, for present purposes, his daughter's opinion is quite good enough for him. Of his two literary children, she has more natural talent, has been at it longer, has read more, and is identifiably the genuine article. He is giving his own view, but he will quote her. This gives his view extra authority, not least in the mind of its intended hearer, and it also exonerates him of any brutal dismissal. But he is sensitive to reputations, and he believes he knows what makes for a woman's good name. He cannot have his own daughter being crude. So he covers up for her. He is probably oblivious to the fact that he has given himself away. The tactic is winning: you can't help but laugh and feel for him an affection that is only slightly pitying, as his own kindness and code combine to trip him up. Yet he insists that reportage and morality are both straightforward affairs.

'The old man's not altogether reliable,' he says. 'Especially when he gets on to nuns. There's something not quite right there.'

'They kept these things quiet,' says the old man. 'No bad thing either. What good would it do, getting into the papers, being gloated over everywhere? They were good women, the vast majority of them, and why should they be tarred with the same brush as the one bad apple? Some people believe the worst of them anyway, so why bother confirming bigotries. Keep it in the family, where there's room for understanding and forgiveness.

'By the time we'd finished at Beaudesert, we needed police and a coroner as well as myself. I had a look at the last one taken sick. Easy enough to tell: arsenic poisoning. She pulled through all right, we'd got there early enough. But the others had shown the same symptoms, so we had to exhume them. There'd been no thought of an autopsy before: a bad bout of gastric trouble, there was no reason why it couldn't kill. Something sinister would never occur to you, not in a convent, not for one illness or even two. But we examined the contents of their stomachs this time, and it was the same thing all right, arsenic.'

My grandfather is not bothering with any sense of climax. All his reflections about scandal and keeping the secret in the family give the game away. The fact he assumes all along is that there is only one place to look for the murderer because convents are self-contained units. To the extent that they are not, they have nullified any possibility of external influence.

The butcher, let's say, a man with vicarious access to the persons of all the nuns, would be chosen on the basis of sympathy. He, as much as the doctor and the police, would be one of the fold. Even if just a very sympathetic Protestant, he would, in terms of discount, a soft spot for the good nuns, nice little cuts, and all the rest of it, be living in harmonious rhythm with them. If, against all the probabilities, he were out of tune and had had some tiff with them without losing their custom or was harbouring a grudge so fierce that it grew to murderous proportions, his problem in moderating the slaughter would be immense. If his animosity were comprehensive, why would he not lace all of one week's meat and be done with it? But he hadn't done that, presumably for one of two reasons. To wipe out the lot at once would be more incriminating than a protracted picking-off of the victims. Or maybe his grievance was particular. But if that were the case, he would surely be up against insuperable problems of nailing the precise victim. How could he ever be sure that the tainted set of kidneys would be consumed by Sister Meretrix, the object of his loathing? No, he could only dose his weekly delivery like that if he didn't care which individuals he caught. And that possibility, a homicidal objection to a whole convent whose custom you still have, flies in the face of common sense.

'They took her down to Sydney,' says my grandfather. 'Your father was at university there at the time, and we sent a telegram asking him to meet the plane. Just Mother Dominica and the nun in question.'

This is speed. From all parties. Cutting corners, ignoring the niceties, not to mention the rules. My grandfather says nothing about motivation or sleuthing. By rights they should be the centre of the story. All those obvious questions that cry out for treatment: why would a nun embark on the eradication of her sisters, of every single one of them perhaps; what link is there between murderous tendency and the scribbling of obscenities on the school blackboard; what would be the first signs; was there an order to the killings; if so, what, or was it random; did the Reverend Mother, or any, or all, of her nuns drop to the culprit the moment foul play was suspected? In a community of fewer than a dozen, where each member is bound to manifest the state of her soul to her Superior every few months, where refusal to do so is unthought of, dissimulation should have been impossible. Before a Superior of any perceptiveness, the chances of hiding derangement or ill-will or any degree at all of being disgruntled with the world should have been nil. To have come up with two and a half murders as a finale to your career in the convent you would, surely, have managed a previous act or two that succeeded in catching the audience's attention. Oddities might be a dime a dozen in religious houses, but sick or dangerous actions should stand out. But, it must be admitted, no number of probabilities will prove that Reverend Mother would have been a wake-up to her sororicidal daughter from the instant the purge got under way. The speculation could go on endlessly: the questions to be asked and the angles of approach are legion.

My grandfather is totally uninterested in them. Other issues take priority. In the first place he is a professional man with an obligation of confidentiality. Thirty years after the event he is still not inclined to give details. Apart from individuals' reputations, the good name of the convent, and the religious order, and the religious state in general would be threatened by the exposition of lurid details and merciless psychiatric diagnosis. My grandfather is honest and faces facts, but playing Maria Monk with her revelations is both alien and distasteful to him.

Secondly, he does not enlarge on the sexual natures or the kinkier proclivities of women. That is not to say he does not pronounce on them. He has apparently assured views – and many of them seem quaint or contradictory, although it is foolish to deride him for that – but he is not willing to enter on an exposition of the evidence, the logical increments that contributed to those opinions. It is not lack of confidence, it is not mere delicacy. It is certainly not an arrogant refusal to back his opinions. Rather, it is a sense that to advance garrulously into that field would be a trespass. Not that what he says is wrong, but to discourse freely on that subject is an infringement on the rights of the owners of the subject as it were. Whether or not they themselves care to exercise that right is another matter. To do so should be up to them. That is the logic of it, but I would be reluctant to claim my grandfather would allow the owners such liberty. He would consider reticence the proper behaviour for women in this matter. It is a complicated and almost casuistical attitude he has, but of course he himself has never formulated it.

'The old man hardly spoke about the nuns at Beaudesert,' says my father. 'Should you?'

'Your father wouldn't believe these sorts of things about consecrated people,' says the old man. 'A very upright fulla, your father. Always was.'

'Did he know what Dominica and her companion were coming down for?'

'You don't confide those sorts of things to the telegraph people.'

Chicken maryland is becoming a memory. It's suited me, and then again it hasn't. Playing the batter and the flesh and the fine, light bones with knife and fork allows for delicate, methodical work, probing, scraping in the interstices of joints, turning the wrist as the scraps of good meat are prised loose. But the dish is antipathetic to vigorous, hungry attack, to uninhibited sawing. Given the rules under which I work – that although chop bones may be taken up in two fingers and picked clean, the same licence does not apply to fowl – chicken maryland is not the raw, unregulated, primeval dish of passion. But I would probably order it again.

I have no idea what the old man is eating.

'Your father told me the end of the story,' he says. 'Thought I might be interested. As a case history as it were. Dominica took the sick woman, the guilty woman – call her what you like – out to . . . what's your place . . . Mount St Margaret, the Blue Sisters – your one for the mentally disturbed. Everything arranged quietly. She'd be out of the way, but among friends with the know-how to cope with her.'

There seems a case here for the champions of the due processes of law. Orangemen, investigative journalists, Masons, royal commissioners, would surely have a field day on this one. My grandfather is unaware of any anomaly. If this is the way criminals can best be neutralised, and those caught up in the event most effectively helped to resume tranquil, productive normality, then this is a legitimate action. Police officers can use discretion, and who is corrupted? No money, no personal advantage is involved. My grandfather sees no problem.

Questions about such a procedure may be very correct, but they're of no interest. Why was this allowed, why did that happen? Of course it's satisfying to pinpoint some efficient cause; a wellspring for the nun's sororicide might be isolated, and the detective, the doctor will squirm with the pleasure of the discovery. But it is nothing to the pursuit of a formal cause that will give an intelligibility to that whole strange set of occurrences. Grasp a shape to this series of events, and the delight is far more suffusive. You have a structure that is pleasing but not necessary; it explains but it can be superseded; it is immanent in the phenomena but all the work of the observer.

'What's the good of philosophy if it's not a philosophy of life,' says my father.

'Life is more than practical, daily actions,' I tell him.

He is impatient with evasion and casuistry. 'What's the good of it except in the eyes of the Almighty? There's a Latin phrase for it, isn't there? You ought to know that. *Sub* something or other'.

'*Sub specie aeternitatis.*'

'Yes, that's it. Under . . . whatever it is . . . the eye of eternity. Only what matters at the moment of death. That's the only philosophy worth bothering about. The one that'll make you ready to die.'

'Of course. But different people have different needs to be satisfied before they're ready to die.'

'Don't give me that. How many people have you seen die? I've seen hundreds, and it's a simple matter of them facing their conscience or not.'

'Well yes, I wouldn't dispute that. My point is that their consciences might be more complex than a few, formal, laid-down codes of conduct. How often is it simply, say, the Ten Commandments that peoples' consciences are worried about?'

'More than you might think, my dear fellow. In fact very rarely not.' My father shifts painfully in his seat preparatory to finishing this with some evidence. 'I had a patient once, a good example, an elderly woman. She was sent to me with shortness of breath, ready fatigue, all the symptoms of cardiomyopathy. Nowadays she'd be an immediate candidate for a transplant, but at that time, 1954 it was, there was nothing I could do. How could you repair and revivify the multiple muscles of the heart? I admitted her to hospital, out at Lewisham, but merely to ease things for her. We just had to leave her to die. Comfort and help her to do that. Nowadays it's a whole new branch of medicine – palliative care. They've got more drugs and the rest of it, but the important thing still remains the attitude and the manner of the doctor. The nurses too, of course.'

'Yes, but what about this woman?'

'She was very unhappy, everyone could tell it. Restless, sleeping very badly, nightmares, unwilling to talk to anyone – you know, not even the few words here and there to the staff. But you didn't interfere: people have got to work it out for themselves, and die in their own way. And you've all got too much to do.'

Anyone can see where this story is going. It's a Catholic cliché. Every priest has a swag of them. The troubled soul facing the death sentence, and the one necessary action is so simple, and yet so difficult. If the soul can just make the break, it is healed instantly and totally. Grace is abounding, waiting only for the nod, the slightest pressure of the wilting hand, to pour into the soul with all the fuel needed for the forced march into eternity. Then it surges on the supererogatory gift of consolation that lifts frailer souls and enthuses them for the road ahead.

'The first bad sign in a convent, or anywhere else,' the old man tells me, 'is maudlin and sentimental piety. It's not healthy, it's not mature, and it can lead anywhere. Puppy love, it's another species of that. Best to get carried off in the throes of it, like Romeo and Juliet, before anything can turn sour and you come down with a thud.'

I'm not aware that I've ever been subject to emotional peaks and troughs, and the warning is rather remote. I lay down my knife and fork, and I hope that my grandfather finds nothing shameful or ridiculous or contemptible about me. I haven't said much, but I hope that my ready ear and sophisticated sense of decorum will give him a feeling for my worth.

I place my knife and fork parallel in the middle of my plate, the handles pointing directly towards my breastbone. I have the prongs of the fork in the convex, closed position. It seems the most elegant placement: an upright, dignified stance over an empty plate, signifying that the user, in spite of the sensual indulgence of eating, has remained in control and asserted the primacy of orderly rationality over carnal destruction. Yet I am worried: I know that the etiquette books are not unanimous on this matter. The convex position, after all, achieves its dignity at the cost of fragility, and therefore smacks of the pretentious. It has a hefty potential to backfire. A waiter removing the plate is as likely as not to topple the fork. Prongs down, it can more easily slide forward and roll onto its back. When it does so it is inevitably with a clatter. Such a ruckus reflects not on the clumsiness of the waiter but on the thoughtless ill-breeding of the plate's user. On the other hand, to position the fork in the open concave position is undeniably safer and more low-key. It is also slightly self-effacing: the fork is not the assertive animal at all; it is the helpless, childish creature on its back shrinking away from notice.

I know that these matters are not unimportant: the choices confirm and strengthen particular dispositions. My trouble is that I am not sure what disposition I should have, or at least which one would be preferable in my grandfather's eyes. He has been talking, he has not yet finished his food, and so he has not yet laid down his cutlery. He is an Irishman, he is foreign, and by definition has vestiges of the barbarian in him. His example may be misleading, or he may expect from me something different to his own practice. So I just have to take the plunge and strike out on my own.

On Christmas morning . . .

That's a lead weight for the beginning of a story. It's a given, and the given should be disposable, but the story refuses to betray its integrity as an old moral tale, and if you inherit a story, free of charge, you've got obligations. Some core respect is non-negotiable. The story comes from those who lived it. It's enough to feed off their lives without a story of my own: I should at least avoid doing violence to them. Besides, I have a weakness for the drama of it.

On Christmas morning, 1954, in the public ward, she drew herself up in her bed. She had not been prepared for centre stage, or for any spotlight. The grey sunless hair shielded her face from any light. The pinched breathing had left no muscle in the face capable of eloquence. She hadn't the awesome presence of being skeletal. It was a pasty, torpid, doughy body that shifted, largely ineffectually, in the bed. No one else in the ward, no nun on duty, took notice. The streamers criss-crossing the ward were motionless. In the crib, beyond her bed, the Christ child lay back in His manger, and held open His arms to the group that were attending on Him.

There was no clearing of the throat, no build-up. The words came in a violent expulsion. There was a poison there that the organism gathered its forces against silently, and then vomited out in one clean purge.

'I am a murderer,' she shouted. The cry was articulated, not shrieked: there was no mistaking the words. 'I am a murderer,' she repeated, and went on repeating. Somehow energy for speech had been conserved during her long silence. There was no elision of the words 'I' and 'am', no sliding over onto that noun, no giving her confession a largely sensational quality. She was defining herself. 'I am a murderer,' she trumpeted to the world. There was no distracting and palliating by using the feminine form of the word. Over and over she began the sentence that the self-portrait is built from, the sentence that can open out into an infinity of descriptions.

'I am a murderer,' she cries. All around they stir, and some stare, and most are embarrassed, and it's no use any of them telling her to keep quiet even if they had the authority. So the confession rings in the air, unrelentingly, for ten minutes. All who witness it are given time for their own self-definition to become a question. 'I am,' the words force their way to the front of every skull lying there, and they tap impatiently on the forehead, waiting to be harnessed to some word that will yank them forward with the bold confidence of individuality. The sick lie there wondering and sometimes dreading what individual will clatter forth and assert possession.

The registrar and the chaplain arrive simultaneously. The medical man has the wisdom to defer, or maybe just the readiness to pass when something is beyond him. As the priest advances to the screaming woman he kisses his stole and places it round his neck. He bends low and comes into her line of vision, and he takes her hand. The cries cut out. He whispers: the expression on his face suggests a question, but the resolute shadow of his body across the bed betrays that his words are an instruction. He pauses, then he blesses her with the sign of the Cross. Her lips move, but this time the only person in the ward who hears her is the priest.

'Well what do you make of that?' says my grandfather.
What's it mean to make something of a story like that?
'Amazing,' I say, 'an amazing coincidence.'
I would like some sweet. I don't know if my grandfather offers
such things.

The
Name
of the
Father

WHEN THE TIME CAME for him to die my grandfather was still uneasy about two people. About his treatment of them. That's my reading of him now, twelve years after his death. I had no such firm view at the time. And doubtless it would be disputed by others who maybe knew him even better. They have a responsibility to him, they argue – their father, their medical mentor, their guide to the secular world. I concede all those bonds, and the debts and responsibilities – and protectiveness – they bring with them. I'm sure there are other connections, with their own rights, that might well demand elbow room in the jostling friction of perspectives. But there are limits too.

For example, no one can speak for him as an uncle. This impossibility defies the odds. Although he had only one sister himelf, and she died at eighteen, his wife was one of ten. This item raises a host of other possible reflections on the family and their values and Ireland which might also be disputed but, as one argument at a time is enough, I simply pick out one bald fact. Of the other nine only one reproduced. This was not due to any high rate of infertility – physiological not statistical infertility – in the family, but to the fact that eight of them never gave it a go. Or at least they didn't do so maritally or even openly – insofar as illicit dipping in the pool of fertility is ever open. Quite simply, eight of them had no recorded offspring. Whether or not they put themselves in the way of even making offspring possible I have no idea. And of course, my even mentioning the matter could be, to some people, a slur. They are not married. Ergo. Well, who am I to say such confidence is more objectionably presumptuous than my allowing for the flesh's itch?

One other of the ten siblings had children. But he was a New York cop. I'm not sure that my grandfather even knew of their existence. I believe it's reasonable to dismiss them as having any legitimate perspective on their uncle. Unless it is that of a Brisbane doctor's total unconcern for the children of a New York cop. But surely that's stretching it. The point is that there *are* other perspectives than mine, but they aren't limitless. The possibilities for the fair picture go only so far.

A fellowship of live and let live has to come into being. Different perspectives on the one old man. So I'm laying my cards on the table, and I call him my grandfather. Any other name or title would suggest I am making more comprehensive claims for my account. I'm not.

He has only two worries. After a ninety-one-year lifetime merely two might seem a light load for his conscience, but the two are his father and his son. At the outset, more or less, I should state that my grandfather is a rational man, not troubled by scruples, not a prey to guilt. The burdens his conscience feel are intrinsic to the code he has evolved himself. He believes he has cause to be troubled by his treatment of his father and his son. He has treated both his past and his future a little unceremoniously. But that's my expression of the regrets, and perhaps it does not allow them a proper gravity. It is one thing to claim rights to my own perspective, but they are still not rights to gratuitous or flippant judgements. My grandfather may be my creation, but too off-hand, too insouciant, too irresponsible a grandfather will besmirch only me, not him. Self-preservation is the guiding principle for this history.

He abandoned his father. So he expresses it in his blacker moments. He reined in his son so tightly that the inevitable breakout was an uncontrollable spiral to destruction. Yet the bonds between my grandfather and his father were close and deliberately reaffirmed in adulthood. Just as you could say that in fact my grandfather let his son run free. Yet the neglect of the one and the disciplining of the other are his retrospective readings of the two losses. Should I confront him with an alternative account, a rehabilitation? Do the ingredients exist for a plausible argument?

Willy-nilly my grandfather was certainly bound to his father; he carried his name, Harry. But because he had no say in that, the bond need have meant nothing more than the most sentimental and superficial of connections. But he made it his own by a gesture of commitment that any evangelist would have been proud to elicit. And no less for its being not the least bit original. By October 1914 he was in Toowoomba. His father was still in Omagh, County Tyrone, and his wife was at the opposite end of that country in the city of Cork, giving birth to a son. It was the old story of Joachim. There she is, surrounded by her relatives – Paddy and Mary-Maggie and Bridie and Nell and Tommy – playing their fiddles to her 'only you, Norah,' and he reaches out, across the barrier of silence that separates them, and imposes a name for his son that, to these Carrolls, is not just new but foreign. 'His name is Harry,' he informs them. With the maximum distance between himself and his own father, he renews the lines of blood. The action is all the starker for its one appearance. The rest of the naming he hands over to his wife. As a second name to Harry she adds Matthew. It's the name of her brother, the older of two priests. The younger one is already in Australia where the mother and child are going, and so his patronage is more readily assured. Uncle Matt, in Ireland, needs a gesture he won't forget. His name is borrowed. So, indirectly, the child is handed over to the guardianship of St Matthew, a reformed merchant banker and end-of-life scribe. With the result that the child, all his life, remains innocent of money matters, and during his last few years he devotes himself to writing up the momentous events of his era. His mother's choice of patron is effective.

Sensing her touch, my grandfather gives her a completely free hand from there on. He is conscientious about his responsibilities, but they are limited. His piety is strictly Roman. Duty towards parents is its chief component. Hers is more conventional turn-of-the-century Irish. But within that pattern she pays off various debts – potential as well as actual. Her daughter, later, she calls Mary. My grandfather's wife is not under discussion at the present, and so I've no business speculating about her motives except to point out that she was thirty-four when they married, and . . . No, that's another question entirely, my grandfather's marriage. I merely note that his daughter got the name Mary, and it was the child's mother's doing. Then the subsequent sons were named: Morgan – for the general practitioner, at the time my grandfather's partner, who delivered him; Gerard – for the patron of pregnancies; and Clem – for a German saint who was nothing much at all, but he was a Redemptorist like Saint Gerard and since she'd started with one religious family why change, and besides the Redemptorists who had her husband's ear as well as her own had no doubt got at her.

'Harry' alone was no statement about his mother. Unless you insist that he spoke eloquently about her sense of precedence and submissiveness. But that would be a fragile deduction. He could equally have been proclaiming her skill at trade-offs, her ability to fall back a pace in order to advance a mile. It would be unjustified to say his name said anything about his mother.

'Your father,' says my grandfather, 'taught me and his brothers what respect for a mother is all about.'

An odd-sounding conversion. An unlikely combination of teacher and lesson. But my grandfather has nothing more specific to say about it. Perhaps he was just looking for, from that son who had been such a gesture of connection with his father, a sign that the gesture was in no way a snub to his wife – especially now that the father was long and well out of his life, whereas the woman seemed set by his side for the long haul.

But it is his father's going out of his life that worries him at the end. As though the pendulum has swung again and, with the wife now twenty years dead, it is the more ancient omissions and commissions that gnaw at him.

He is standing with his father on the wharf in Sydney. 'It's not you, you must know that,' says his father, and he is looking seawards towards the gangway. 'You know,' he says, 'I could live with you under a cart.'

My grandfather takes the phrase, holds it firmly, and feels the unseen heat of it. He cannot cry out, he cannot throw it away. And the words cut down into him, and stay there. And his father has gone.

His father's business is the injection and knifing and parturition of large animals. His active recreation is the mounting of heavy hunters and the racing of them headlong across the stone walls and ditches of Ireland. His ornaments are the photographs and sketches of the celebrated pugilists of his generation and the one before. And now the last words that he says to his only son, his only child, are as unromantic *and* as full-blooded a declaration of affection as one could make. He has not lived with his son for twelve years, and he knows he will never live with him again. But they could live together, he says, under a cart. Call it eccentric, but this is a confession of absolute love, a marriage vow unelicited by the formal demands of a ceremony and set text. And the father goes while the son is catching his balance from the unexpectedness and the plenitude of it. But the son is off balance and branded for the rest of his life. The father could live with him anywhere, but didn't. Maybe, actually, he couldn't. And maybe it was the son's doing.

I say to my grandfather, 'Why wouldn't he stay? There must have been some compelling reason. After all he'd made that long voyage to be with his wife, his only child, the only grandchild he had then. And he'd be going back to live without any of them, never, likely enough, to see them again.

'It was the horses,' says my grandfather, 'the way they treated the horses here. So he said. And I wouldn't say it wasn't the reason.'

My grandfather goes into a brown study. He seems as puzzled as I am by this disproportion between cause and effect.

'We'd the ticket booked for the train to Toowoomba, and while he was in town he went one day to William Inglis's Newmarket stables. Out there near the racecourse, Randwick. I believe it's still there. He never got over it. Said he couldn't stay or work in a country where they treated horses so cavalierly, no . . . so unprofessionally as they did there.'

'It's supposed to be the best, *the* place. T.J. Smith outlays millions there at every yearling sale they have.'

'Is that so now?' My grandfather registers the fact and there's even a strong rhythm of interest in his voice. And it does mirror the mind even while it's reflexive. So that he can return to his train of thought without even a hiccup. 'It's what he was used to, what we were both used to in Omagh. You didn't sell a horse by leading him around in a ring where he was gaped at by any number of people who'd no interest in him.'

'That's what your father thought?'

'He did. At home it was the vendor and the buyer and the vet standing between them and the horse under the hands of all of them.' My grandfather takes in the symmetry of the scene. 'He loved a horse. He couldn't see them treated anything less than royally. He had that . . .' My grandfather rubs the tips of his fingers together. 'He had that feeling of obligation. A horse in the family. The stables were at the side of the house. Mr McArdle was the groom. The only person we employed. No one in the house. No one for my mother. But Mr McArdle was a valet and housemaid to the horses. I'd stand to watch him in the evenings when he'd dusted and washed and brushed and watered and fed them all and when he'd swept out the stables. I stood at the gate onto the street, and I watched him as he moved along the rows of them saying his goodnight to each set of hindquarters, giving every animal the attention of a different word and a different voice – but all the while his eyes sharp before and behind him for the first uneasy stirring and the lifting of a tail. And if he saw it, he leaped and danced to the disturbed horse with such quiet agility that none of the others was startled or even noticed it. And he took up his place as the sphincter loosened and the anus expanded, and his hands were there in a wide mobile bowl as the hot steamy gobbets came up into view and rolled out with the precision and speed of an assembly line. And Mr McArdle did his jig on the cobbles as his hands rolled to and fro, towards and away from the crupper, under the rearing mound of golden dung. Never once, never once,' says my grandfather, 'did I see him drop even one . . . one link in that labile chain. There was no . . . no mess in any of the stables when Mr McArdle closed the gate on the stable yard for the night, and I went inside.'

That's where the free flow of my grandfather's pondering leads him. Mr McArdle and his juggling. And I wonder whether he hasn't given his answer, and gone on past it, into apparent irrelevance, to throw me off the scent of any other, more awkward, explanation. The old man could live with his son under a cart, but what of the others? All this lyricism, is it to distract me away from something?

'He was active still,' says my grandfather. 'What was there for him in this country?'

But is Mr McArdle there when the old man goes back? Are the hunters? Does his supervision of knowledgeably conducted sales compensate him for the total loss of a family? Or at least a son? Probably not. The return to the old country brings out – maybe just exacerbates – a drinking problem. He can't do without family. He retires to Cookstown, to his brother's, a tailor. He writes to his son in Toowoomba, asking him to return and visit him. But for his son there is a war on, a new country to be accommodated, a practice to be built up, a mother and a wife and two sons now to be supported. The old man has to be left alone.

But he doesn't lose his professional pride or his flair. Not entirely. Three years before my grandfather dies I meet a man, a small farmer, a grandson of the tailor, my grandfather's cousin and mine too. He has been born with a club foot and wears a boot raised some inches, and he also has a contracted muscle in his hand. But he has spent a lifetime handling his plough. The old man, the vet, had been in the household when he was born. He examined the condition; he said it was just a matter of snipping certain muscles. He himself could do it, he would be happy to do it. I feel my grandfather's conscience might be eased by this initiative, that he might derive from it the consolation that he had not remotely killed the spirit of his father. That the old man had remained confident his professional edge was at its very keenest.

'And this fulla was still lame, you say?' My grandfather is only interested in the facts of the medical history. 'Did the old man botch it, did he?'

'No, no.' I have to tell him the rest of the story. 'The child's mother considered the offer. Finally she said no.'

'Good woman,' says my grandfather. 'The old man was neat with his knife, but a vet has no business operating on babies. Kindness and enthusiasm and the sense of being under an obligation must have got the better of him. Sensible woman saying no to him.'

'It wasn't that at all actually. Do you know what she said to him?'

'Tell me.'

'She said, "That's the way God sent him into the world, and that's the way he'll go out of it."'

My grandfather nods his head. He's heard it before. 'Great motto for the medical profession that one.' He turns and looks at me. It is stern exasperation. 'Benighted country'.

And he lost his own father back into it. So completely that he doesn't know when or where he died, where he was buried. There has been no avoiding regrets. There has been no alternative for the solitary, meditative man but to scout around for the paths that he might have followed and inspect their viability. 'I can't tell you how much I enjoy your visits,' this severe old grandfather says to me, and the tears are there. 'Stops me thinking. These long nights are terrible. I can't stop thinking.' He asks me to return as soon as I can and he gives me money – to cover the train fare, to control at least that conveyance. For the noise of the great machines is the score to his nightmares. The liner, sliding away from Circular Quay, hooting above the silent, awesome vacuum expanding between ship and wharf, and above the white vortices starting up in the green water, spinning father and son away from one another.

And rising above that is something far more terrible: the high, shrill crescendo, engines and the rush of air, of the Beaufort going down, taking the Brisbane boy towards the utterly foreign grave of the North Sea. My grandfather sees Gerard, his son, spiralling away from him. He wants to know what has happened: is it engine failure, is there some other human being there, some young German who has got the better of his son this time as his son had got the better, three weeks before, of another young man, a Heinkel pilot and sent him down into the sea? My grandfather wonders whether his son has gone through the gladiatorial routine of a dogfight, concentrated by the chilling certainty of killing or being killed, or whether he has been taken unawares out of the sun and out of the cloud, or whether he has seen the tracers coming, or whether the bullets have entered his own body or his own head first or whether unscathed he has been carried down by a stricken aircraft. My grandfather doesn't want to know; it is more that some knowledge wants to force itself on him. He wants to grasp the boy, hold him, stop him. But the boy slides through and away, out of sight.

'I was too hard on him,' says my grandfather.

'Gerard liked dressing up, night clubs, that sort of thing,' says my father.

'His death was the end of his mother,' says my grandfather.

Gerard was her sacrificial son, dedicated to the saint who, if anyone, would be her guardian from any more miscarriages. This was the son who would be the token of God's special solicitude for mothers. But the saint had let him too slip from her, a welter of blood and collapsing sac. She shuffled and hovered through fifteen years, seeking in the narrowing spaces of her own mind the boy who went down.

So my grandfather sees a cycle of disintegration in his family, and he tries to gauge and assess his degree of responsibility for it. He does not wallow, beat his breast, tear his hair, even veer towards hysterical upset or breakdown, but nor does he harden himself against the possibility that he was somewhere blameworthy.

'He must have been out looking for that big ship they were all scared of . . . what was its name?'

'The *Bismarck*.'

'That's the one.'

My grandfather pauses, shrugs just slightly. Is it worth saying any more? Saying the obvious? 'Just never came back. Shot down I suppose. Into the sea.' And my grandfather falls into a reverie.

I am stilled by his words. This is how a father speaks of the death of his own son. With apparent dispassion. With laconic directness. With untrembling precision. He follows him down, unswerving, to the bottom. The child he was presented with in the hospital nursery, the child cut loose from its mother and accepted by him as its main supporter and protector. I am awed by this distilled calm.

I would prefer not to look, but I cannot help it. I have not lost a child given to me. I can afford to run my horrified but insatiable mind through all the ironies of a child presented and a child ripped away. But my grandfather holds the image of his son's death squarely, and arraigns himself as its cause.

'When he wanted to leave school I sent him back.'

'That wouldn't have done him any harm.'

'He was mechanically minded. Wanted to do things with his hands. Loved tinkering.'

'He could have done that at the same time as . . . whatever else.'

'I thought we'd got the family up out of all that. The old man had done that sort of thing. While he was doing his veterinary science, he worked in the shipyards.'

'Then it must have been in the blood.'

'Surgery was what I thought was in the blood. His father, his grandfather, both his elder brothers.'

'Well, his hands might have adapted to that if you'd been able to hold them there long enough.'

'He ran away. I set the police to look for him.'

'Any father would have done that, should have done that.'

'It was his own brother, your father, they got to identify him. By his feet first. In mechanic's overalls. Sticking out from under some car in a garage in Wentworth Avenue down in Sydney.'

'But he went quietly. He must have wanted to be found.'

'But if he'd been left there with the cars, he'd never have taken up flying lessons.'

'The one would very likely have led to the other.'

'His mother went tight with worry. She waved to him, you know that, every time he went up. She took a blanket onto the verandah on Gregory Terrace and when she heard him she flapped it up and down, as violently and as extended as she could, and he came in low over the house, lower than he should've, I'm sure, and when he saw the blanket flapping he dipped his wings to it and then off again.'

'That must have been marvellous.'

'She was terrified for him. Told herself that if she could give him a wave like that he'd be safe. Half-believed that flapping the blanket shooed away whatever evil little people were up there in the air with him.'

'No, she must have enjoyed it. How many other women were able to say hello to their sons like that?'

My grandfather turns his head half side-on to me. 'She wasn't saying hello to him at all. Whatever she might have thought she was doing, she was saying goodbye to him . . . I should never have let him up there. I should never have paid the money.'

'Well then you can hardly blame yourself for keeping him on too tight a rein.'

'Why else would he have shot into the sky like that except the pressure that had built up?' My grandfather swings his chin forward a couple of times. It's resigned inevitability. 'Then he has his pilot's licence, then the war comes. How can he be stopped? Victoria, Canada, somewhere in England, the North Sea. And his mother comes apart, slowly. And two of the other boys are in the army, and

I have to stop the last one from following. And I have a medical practice to keep going.' He speaks without self-pity. Rather, he enumerates what turns into a list of compensations. 'And then,' he says, 'three months later your father gets married.'

So the child that got his grandfather's name, which happened also to be the name of his father, is not going to make too craven an obeisance to death. He is getting on with it, he says. And when he has a son he abandons the tradition of his fathers and does not consider the name Harry. Maybe he has forgotten where he came from. Twice he has made a new start, leaving Ireland as a boy, leaving Queensland as an undergraduate. Again there is a war on, and it is a professional rather than a family future that absorbs him. But his code too would have to be called classical, and so it includes a strong filial *pietas*. There has been a loss to the family, a gap has appeared, and when my father adds a new male to the family he is restoring the loss, and so he calls the child Gerard.

Forty years later, grandfather dead and father dying, I have a son, and we call him Harry.

My Father's Version of the Nurses' Story

FIRST THE WAR, then medicine, came between my father and myself. In my first years and his most receptive years, my father had more things to do than hang around attending to me. He went to war, he went to the Royal College of Surgeons. I stayed behind. He had chosen his ground, and I wasn't on it, then or ever.

So now, each from the safety of his own territory, my father and I circle around one another. We don't have much time and the questions are pressing. My father wants desperately to be proud of his children. I have reservations about his criteria, but I cannot resent the wish. He is becoming less certain about this writing business. He has always thought it an amateur affair – an after hours activity anyone should be able to do. He has been writing all his life, he says, dozens and dozens of articles in medical journals. But now I hear him say, 'My son is a writer.' Old friends and colleagues tell him when they read something I write and find it marginally comprehensible. He offers no opinion himself. But he offers me subject matter. 'Come and see this operation,' he says. 'You might like to write about it.'

He holds in his hand something I have written, and gestures with it. But he comments by way of something similar that happened to himself, or by recalling his presence at some event I have mentioned. He does not engage. Not that I demand he should. His feints are quite eloquent enough. He'll come closer in his own good time, I think. He has his own approach, his own style.

He comes at me obliquely. I approach him more directly. My strongest pull is to what is most foreign to me. There are possibilities there, I tell myself. I accept his invitation to go into the operating theatre. I check with him on medical details. I quiz him on symptoms and diagnoses and prognoses.

And I ask him about the war. I have not been to war. So I wonder and wonder about it. And I badger my father terribly about his war. I envy him. Tell me about a medical war, I ask him. Make something of it, I want to tell him. It must be a great clarifier. So my endeavours converge; I probe at the man, and I stick out my finger into the maelstrom.

I don't want any of the clichés, ancient or modern, about war. I know all that, I don't need a father for it. I keep prodding him on this event or that. I hope the individual will suddenly stand forth. But it's not easy going, getting the apocalyptic story out of him. He is ready to be dry, laconic.

I prompt him with a photo album, and he does his tour of duty round the south-west Pacific. In the Ramu Valley he peers at thousands of glass plates, trying to identify the malaria bacillus in swabs taken from sick troops carried out of the jungle. He is warned not to be fooled by the fly shit. In Singapore he leads Lord Louis Mountbatten on a tour of his wards in the Fourteenth Australian General Hospital, and he says, 'I am just to the left outside the picture,' or 'I am standing just beside the photographer.' So he is not recorded with royalty.

I try to nudge him further towards the centre of things. 'Was most of the work with battle casualties?' I ask. 'No,' he says, 'mostly not.' And I think he is going to leave it at that. But he begins again. 'But the worst moment was . . . I suppose you could call it that . . . "battle casualties". We were waiting in Moresby. The paratroopers had taken Nadzab. We were to fly there soon, but before we went more infantry had to follow up. They were waiting in a marshalling yard at the end of the runway. A Liberator, loaded with bombs and petrol, took off. It clipped a tree, staggered, and crashed beside a company of the waiting infantrymen. They were doused in burning petrol. We worked frantically. We cleaned the skin, removed the blisters, covered with vaseline gauze. We had rows of starkly red, shiny bodies. It was a terrible thing to do in the light of what we now know. They were literally flayed alive. Every one of them died.' My father is matter of fact. He can live with that. He has never had nightmares. Medicine has advanced. And medicine will never know very much. My father must have the perfect temperament for surgery. He has not a callous nerve in his body, but no amount of putrid or flayed or mashed flesh has ever disabled him. All right, I say, a person can live with that. The images of the inferno are never likely to dull; they are not, God help us, uncommon. Nor even necessarily unsettling. They're on vicarious offer far too readily.

So I see no alternative but to move towards the most dangerous topic. The nurses' story is potentially his best one. But it's islanded amid reefs of sentimentality. And I refuse to be taken in by the merely sentimental. It's my father's besetting sin, sentimentality. I'm determined it won't be the final fruit we harvest from his war. But he's wary too, and I wonder if it's for the same reason. 'How did you come to be involved with the nurses?' I ask.

'Oh, it's in that book there,' he says, with as much amusement as pride, and he points to the shelf. 'You can read it all there.' It's Betty Jeffrey's *White Coolies*. He gets two mentions. It says he was there 'also'. And it says he told those POW nurses there was a ward ready. That's all. But there's more to it than that. The story absorbs me, and I can't believe it's meaningless to him. And I desperately hope that, for both of us, its strength is not as a tear-jerker. I hear it again on the radio, Tim Bowden's 'Just an Ordinary Bunch of Women', and I thank God I'm in a room by myself for I walk around trying to blink back the tears and biting my lip and barely able to restrain myself from sobbing. It's terrible. And I think, is there any way we can end that story, any way we can climax it without making the likes of the pair of us cry?

I don't want to let him build up the pathos of it. He'll give me the sinking of the *Vyner Brooke* and the machine-gunning of the survivors. So I prompt him, 'What was your part in it all at the end?'

'Oh, it was hardly more than a formality really,' he says. He seems unwilling to get started.

'Well, how did you get mixed up in it?' I try.

'I was just told to. Sam Langford, our commanding officer, told me there'd been reports of these nurses somewhere in Sumatra, and I was to locate them.' He is deliberately flat. It's not that he can't tell a story. He is simply dragging his feet, shying away from getting properly into motion.

'All the sisters attached to our C.C.S. had been among the lucky ones to escape from Singapore on the *Empire Star*. They spoke almost daily of their colleagues who had embarked on the *Vyner Brooke*. I knew so many of the names, I knew so many of the personalities. And now I was told to locate them.' My father thinks about that for a while, but doesn't say anything more about it. I'm glad. It's one of those points where the tears could well up very readily.

'We flew to Palembang. We circled twice over the runway, with its Zeros lined up on either side. The Japanese were courteous, wanted to know our business, offered us Kool cigarettes. They showed us to staff cars and drove the seven miles into town. On the way other staff cars met us coming in the opposite direction. The officers in each case would signal to one another by twirling a sheathed sword through the window. The other car would join in behind us. We entered Palembang in a procession of ten staff cars. Japanese troops by the roadside stood at the salute.'

'A special dispensation of providence,' I suggest.

A tremor, part puzzlement, part frown, moves across my father's face. I know he has no time for the intellectual gloss to his stories, but in his own way I think he'd agree with the point. I explain. 'I mean it was a very fitting detail that the nurses could have been liberated in style.'

'I suppose so,' mutters my father, but without any conviction, and as though he hasn't really heard me. I wonder myself whether it isn't a fatuous remark, and my father accepts it only because this is a pitfallen road he is travelling down, and he'll latch on to anything to prevent him slipping into one of his own emotional holes.

Hell, I rebuke myself, it's one feature of the story that's as valid as any other. I could even argue that this wryly ironic climax forces itself on you.

'The nurses weren't in Palembang,' says my father, as though he's suddenly remembered why he takes exception to my gloss. 'We sent out our co-pilot in one of the staff cars, south-west, further into southern Sumatra. He found them, sent word to me, and got them to Lahat where there was a small airstrip. I immediately signalled Matron Sage. She was Matron-in-Chief. She had flown up from Australia and was waiting in Singapore for word of the girls she had inducted into the army.'

My father pauses. This is one of the danger moments. He can't help milking the emotion in the story. I want to hurry him on. But then I wonder whether I'm not just damming back the emotion for a spectacular finale, whether I'm not nervous that he's going to dissipate it bit by bit along the way. Beneath that, I think, I must be wondering whether he realises the potential and proper shape of his story. No, I say to both of us, it doesn't have to be a runaway tear-jerker. Let's just stick to the barest facts, and see what emerges.

'What did she do?' I ask.

'She decided to leave at once to meet them. She flew into Palembang and I was back there to meet her. She had a mishap which I'll always remember.'

I seize on this. 'Why? What happened?'

'As her plane landed it blew a tyre. It had to be taken off, repaired, blown up again, and replaced. I had with me a chap by the name of Chisholm, a sergeant, and an ex-POW. We'd picked him up in Palembang, and I don't know whose, if anyone's, orders he was under. But he took charge of this repair job. He lined up twenty of the Japs and got them to work on the hand pump. As each one tired, Chisholm gave him a push on the arse with his boot, and the next in the queue took over.'

Well, well, I think, here's something to deflate the story.

My father is chuckling. It seems rather distasteful to me. I would like it to be a large comic moment, but it refuses to slip into that shape. The picture I see is of Australian jackboots blasting, in a great shower of sparks and stars, wizened, malevolent, pear-shaped Japanese pygmies all over the sky. Stock figures, a stock picture, that won't fit in with the dignity of the saga. But then maybe that's all the story needs to save it from the gross sentimentality of the likes of my father and myself.

'He was remarkably gentle,' says my father. 'I don't know what sort of life he'd had as a POW, but this way of getting his own back was heckuva mild. He was a bit of an actor, Chisholm. Being nasty to the Japs didn't seem to be in his mind at all. He only had the one old hand pump, and he just used the most efficient method he could. Nobody got hurt or worked too hard; that would have defeated the purpose of it. He just liked the experience once again, at long last, of being in charge and able to give orders. Getting his dignity back. So he posed and strutted a bit, and generally over-acted the part. But with a healthy twinkle in his eye the whole time.' My father chuckles, remembering Chisholm.

If my father insists that's the way it was, I don't see how I can make anything else out of it. I don't see how I can stop the acceleration at this point. My father seems quite happy now to go on. 'We took off as soon as the tyre had been fixed. The flight took twenty-five minutes. As the plane landed we could see a group of people sitting under an awning on the edge of the strip.'

That's good. He's very matter of fact.

'They didn't stand up. They didn't wave. There weren't very many of them. It wasn't one of those delirious, crowd-scene arrivals at all. They waited. We taxied through the long grass. We could hear it hissing against the undercarriage, through the roar of the engines and the rumble of the wheels. We wobbled to a halt. The co-pilot pushed open the door, and the ladder went down. I stepped out.'

'You stepped out first?'

'Yes.'

'Why did you step out first?'

'Heavens, boy, it was instinctive.'

'Yes, but why?'

'Because that's what you do in those sorts of circumstances. I wasn't just going through any old sort of door. Damn it all, if it's dangerous or difficult or a man can be of some use, he goes first. Doesn't he?' My father brushes aside the triviality of it.

'Yes, I suppose so.' I give up trying to direct him.

'Matron Sage got out. I stood back. I thought she should go first. And she walked . . .'

My father stood back. He thought Matron Sage should go first. I am seized by the off-hand detail. But any man of any sensitivity would have done that, I tell myself. Oh yes! I am answered. Look at the pressure he resisted without any forethought, any tensing himself. So I look at them. He is keyed up. He is first off the plane and has a head's start. He is the senior man. He has been in charge of locating and rescuing these women. He has now arrived to liberate them. He knows all the details of what to tell them, of what arrangements have been made for them. He is a doctor and they are nurses. He is a man and his instincts must prompt him to play the gallant deliverer. And he is a young man and these are young women. But my father stands back.

And Matron Sage walks towards her girls. They are wraiths, they are like the spirits in prison that Christ visited. And now at last they rise up. And the long grass opens and Matron Sage moves towards them, her daughters, and you can hear the sobs bursting through her outstretched arms. She stands there in her felt hat and her grey jacket and grey trousers and takes each of her daughters to her breast. And she asks the echoing question of those months, 'And where are the others?', and of course they give the echoing answer, 'This is all of us, Matron'. And Matron Sage and the girls stare at the incomprehensible horror and joy of it all.

And my father stands back, and tries to stand further back, but he cannot. He is forced to watch and hear everything, and he cannot get away to any other spot. He is forced to hear these words and see these tears. He does not want these tears, but he cannot escape them. They have staked out this plot. It belongs to them alone. And willy-nilly I am tied to him and caught also. It's no good, no good at all. My father and I sit there and cry away together. Other people falter on the edge of the room, and go away again.

De Motu Cordis

'DO YOU MIND BLOOD?' asked my grandfather.

I was being tested for the profession. I had to treat the question as rhetorical. No admission of squeamishness was expected. It would have been foolish and forever alienating to make one. Of course I had no idea what I felt about blood.

My sister was being asked too. 'I don't know. I might,' she said.

So she was stood outside, in the scrubbing room, and told to watch through the glass.

Why should I mind blood? The expression is as curious as the emotion. What is blood doing in the company of such refined dispassion? 'Do you mind?' we are asked, and at worst we reply that, yes, we do rather mind. In any case the expectation is that we won't mind, and not-minding, far from being a positive state, is little removed from apathy or the lackadasaical. It is a passionless, relative world we have arrived at when we use the language of minding. The expression is so little capable of containing strong emotion itself that to declare we certainly have a view or a taste in the matter we must throw our emphasis entirely onto the auxiliary 'do'.

So effete an expression then is all the stranger a bedfellow for a term such as 'blood'. For all the connotations of blood are squarely opposite to lukewarm and wishy-washy and placid. Hence the expression 'do you mind' acquires, just this once, some muscle when it is paired with 'blood'. Its meaning in fact is changed. 'Do you mind blood?' should be read as 'Do you have an aversion to blood?' But the understatement is maintained, so that we enter into a pretence that facing blood is only one of the many trivial confrontations of life.

As indeed it is. We should only 'mind' things that are alien to us, whereas with blood we are in perfect partnership.

The relationship however does have elements of a pretence. A man might be comfortable with his body, but never with his blood. A woman has a better chance, but only superficially. We are comfortable only with what is predictable. Blood might be warm, tangy, exciting, flamboyantly rich, but it is also unreliable and promiscuous. It races when you neither wish nor expect it to, it is quiescent when your heart or your brain – or is it some other faction of the blood itself – aches for some tidal surge from it. It is quirky and volatile. Yet not infinitely so. If it were, that would give it a predictability it refuses to have. So mercurial a nature is beyond us.

We speak, impertinently, of blood belonging to us, but how distant it remains. At the most we might feel its teasing movement passing under our finger, gliding off, just a film of flesh beyond reach. The organs and the bones might be invisible, but they are set and riveted, and some of the organs can even be felt and massaged in their cages. They do not prise themselves loose and erupt. But blood, constantly and inevitably, breaks free. It will allow us the greater intimacy of seeing it, but only when it is escaping from us. Only then can we touch it, and the one gesture we are allowed is not a caress but the blunt unlovely application of a dab, a suck, a staunch. These are the coarse movements of panic, the unscientific, unfamilial gestures of merely coping with what is beyond us. Even then we are torn between affection – or more likely a compulsion towards a show of affection – and we kiss the blood, draw it into ourselves, through the licit and homely opening that we believe is the passage to our true self. Or in distaste we poke and jab at the blood, forcing it back into its bolt-hole, jamming some crude lid down on an opening that shouldn't exist so that the blood will fall back, back, away from view to its proper, unruffling invisibility.

A dicey business, facing blood. We would prefer not to do it directly. So we mind it all right. We make sure that blood doesn't run wild, that it stays in its own playground, and remains contented. We are minders in a violent world. There is something about blood – its richness, its teasing determination to stay just beyond reach – that makes it so vulnerable. We hover about, protective, ready to ward off the blows. We cringe at the thought of blood exposed and suffering. We mind blood terribly.

I stood on the stool, my mask as tight as I could tie it.

My grandfather took the scalpel, poised it, and drew. The blood marked a straight line along the surface of the skin in the wake of the blade. The line developed blotches and a waver. But it remained recognisably a line, untidy not chaotic. Controlled in this way blood was not riotous, yet the pinpricks and the droplets of it blossoming everywhere betrayed that flesh was full of wells of it, wells quite ready to force their way up and flood out across the visible world.

My grandfather had not lost touch with the letting of blood. He was careful with the element, not prodigal but not afraid to release it either. He still felt the salty scarlet rain falling as he knelt on the leg of the colt and his father sliced decisively into the animal's scrotum, and it bucked, and the blood hissed and jetted for an instant into the cold Irish sky, and the father and the son on their knees there together were spattered in its fall.

My grandfather's index and middle fingers straddled the excision and the scalpel went deeper. The line vanished, gullies opened, and pods of blood appeared and held, or burst open and slithered on the honeycomb walls of fat. The assistant dabbed with the gauze pad. Momentarily the blood was broken down and absorbed. My grandfather's fingers slid, jerkily, under the wall and away into the interior. They jiggled themselves into a position where they could grasp and then withdraw the one thing they wanted. Around the base of the fingers the blood regrouped, and the wound called attention to itself again. Fresh globules exploded into sight and then slipped erratically into the gutter. Beneath this raw fever the sheathed fingers twisted and pulled. The scalpel, the gauze, the needle and thread all flashed. The walls began to close, the blood was reabsorbed into them, the skin was knitted up.

In his forceps my grandfather held up a small asymmetrical organ. It was an appendix. The shape of it alone betrayed it as an excrescence. So that surgery was the clean excision of the superfluous, the extrusion, the untoward growth. My grandfather dropped the appendix on to a gauze pad in a kidney bowl.

I had not been sick. I had not even felt like being sick.

Not for years have I seen such a young woman naked. The breasts sit steady with all the natural uprightness of youth, not even tempted into a weary, deflated slide. The belly is unwrinkled and flat, almost concave, above the proud pubic bone. She has her legs tidily together, but the pose suggests not so much modesty as contained energy and purposefulness. Her legs are bathed, smooth and unblemished.

It is the body I look at first. She is naked, I am fully clothed, and in that unequal stance of vulnerability and power you look at the body – hardly out of concupiscence, but rather out of delicacy. You avoid the embarrassment you imagine would be entailed by looking the woman in the face, in the eye. It does not alter my reflex that her eyes are closed. Spontaneously I act as though she might open them at any moment and catch me staring impertinently at her. You do not leave yourself naked like that, the door ajar, your room full of the bright machinery of life, your hands extended and open by your side, your chest rising and falling evenly, unless you are just waiting to be touched so that you can yield yourself to someone's pleasure which, you imagine, can only also be your pleasure.

I know I am an intruder. I have nothing to offer her. But I will not fall into the easy self-castigation of calling myself a voyeur. I do not try to hide the fact that I am observing her. She is off-limits as an object of desire, even in all her beauty. I am too awed to take pleasure. She is quite perfect in the grace of her lines and the nobility of her pose. Only by leaning forward, more intimately than her bearing welcomes, do I see that she has one flaw, on the right side of the neck, almost hidden by the shadow of the chin, the discolouration of a long bruise. My heart circles on and on through a cycle of reverence and winded horror and dumb outsider's grief.

They have a conversation about blood, my father and the surgeon of the donor team.

'I don't like the look of the x-ray,' says the latter. 'Have you seen it?'

'Not yet.'

'The bleeding inside the chest wall is extensive.'

'We've both seen a lot of that. It needn't stymie us.'

'It looks bad.'

'It doesn't mean the heart's not okay.'

'Of course, but the chances are slimmer if the chest wall is awash.'

'Well, funnily enough, no. We did an article, remember, on chest wall bleeding. Not once, do you remember, did we find the heart had been affected?'

It seems to me a curious conversation. My father, retired and stricken with cancer, is there as a courtesy, but this exchange is no mere gesture towards making him feel involved. He is confident and steadying, lulling a disquiet he has scientific reason to believe is unnecessary. This operation is not his, but his hand is evident in it.

But if his authority takes me by surprise I am equally thrown by the intelligibility of what is being said. This is not the precise, technical language of master performers, so sure-footed and esoteric that it becomes impossible to follow. Rather, this brief passage of words is faltering and transparent.

'There's a lot of blood there, I see that,' says my father, 'but I wouldn't be panicked.'

He's impressive. I seize on evidence of my father's impressiveness. Imperturbable, sought out, deferred to – and with reason. Good things for a harshly judging son to see.

I wonder – but I could never ask him – about blood finding its equilibrium. How much blood can there be before there is too much? Before the eyes are clouded by it, or the gasping lungs drowned by it, or the conduits to the heart burst by it? Yet, equally, how small an amount before there is too little? Before the body dries up and shrivels and rots?

She is lifted and swung across the threshold by not one, but two theatre attendants. She is taken from her own bed and placed, naked, in a new one. Her life, or what remains of it, is now for someone else. All the welcomers and well-wishers and the invokers of fertility, of new life striking, and also the merely curious, surround her.

The analogy goes on and on. I have seen a young woman, naked and prepared. Look at the surgeon now. Is he the matriarch, sprinkling the bed and its occupant, driving away the spirits, praying that the seed take? Or is he the priest, anointing the body, smoothing it for its passage into another life?

He takes the sponge, dips it in a kidney bowl, fills it with iodine, and starts to swab her. He moves down from the shoulders. The breasts wobble only slightly as he brushes them. He moves down, generous with the ointment, across the plain of the belly, leaving a small unsettled pool in the navel, and onto the top of the thighs. He skirts the pubic hair, refusing to inflict the indignity of an extended arm and a pair of forceps being poked and fluttered towards the gentials.

'Let's see if we can do a combined harvest,' he says, and turns for his own implements.

The men move in, each to his own plot. There is something for everyone, the cardiac surgeon, the renal surgeon, the hepatic surgeon. They tap probingly on the clay before them; they glance up and around and catch one another's eyes above the mask, and murmur.

'Ready? We'll go right down the centre then?' says the cardiac surgeon.

My father tugs me by the arm. 'This is the part of the whole business that people find hardest to take.'

As I turn away the cardiac surgeon selects the point, high on her perfect chest. He takes the pressure with his scalpel. Again the breasts just barely shudder. The surgeon leans forward, and eviscerates her.

At a certain point you realise the material you have is a goer. There have been alternative possibilities. One by one they have been discarded. Too slight, too short on reserves to last any distance, too wedded to its origins to make a transition, too overused already. You sense this one has simply got the potential, and must be used now or never. You make a grab for it, pluck it out. It is ragged, still smarting. It looks lumpy. It has to be trimmed, all sorts of now-extraneous pendules snipped off. A new resting place has to be found for it. It has to be first sewn, and then absorbed into a new organism, so that it is not merely a parasitical or ill-adjusted guest, but the animating heart of the new body. Let this germ unsettle the flesh that closes round it, and let the two of them wrestle and even savage their way towards some sort of accommodation. Just hold on while they're at it, ease the pressure here, tighten the stitch there. There is no guaranteeing any issue into unified harmony. The enterprise might fall apart, very dirtily and dispiritingly. You might find yourself looking at an expanse of waste and ruined possibilities. You will know there was a chance of jubilant life, and the failure is your doing every bit as much as any success would have been.

But you may come good too. Fuse all those foreign bodies perfectly, and shake your head in wonder at how well all the grafts have taken and what an original, lively animal you have, finding its own independent, wayward place in a world that, likely as not, won't even be your world. There'll be no saying quite what the impact for good or evil will be of this new species. But it's there, and what you've made it from will soon not even be history, so totally absorbed will the past be into this future you have decided.

'It's a matter-of-fact business,' says my father. 'You won't see any flamboyance here. No showing off, no trying to be clever.'

He is right. The place is efficient and low key. Brisk when it has to be, but briskness only comes in bursts. Friend stands beside friend, and spinning half around, arms folded, he smiles, as he makes a jerky comment. Nurses more fixed in their waiting posts, more inscrutable, more consciously but less openly assessing the doctors than the doctors are assessing them. Under the green gowns and Breughelian bonnets no one is striking or even attractive. This is no kingdom of the demi-god. There is no part of the performance that calls attention to itself.

'All right, we'll go with her,' says the man who decides such things.

So they wheel in the woman, only half-sedated because they might have decided not to go with her. A mother, in her thirties, naked only during the few moments when they transfer her from trolley to table. Noises, maybe moans, maybe shards of speech, coming from her restless head. They are going to slice open her chest, take the electric saw to her sternum, clamp back her chest wall, sever the moorings of her heart, prise it out, shrunken and exhausted, and leave her momentarily suspended there with an oval cavity between her lungs. While somewhere there will be a man and small children in an agony of hope. She is lean, even elegant and her body only a little worn, but it does nothing for her that the only thing she is given to wear as she comes to the table is a plastic shower cap. As she is lowered, her relaxed head falls back, and the shower cap slips, barely holding, to the crown of her head. My father, a dying man, takes a short step forward and pulls the cap back into place. He smooths and tucks the straight hair under the rim, and gently slides his fingers back along the elastic, lifting it over the ears. He leans over the woman, and murmurs – words for her only – and as he straightens up he caresses her lightly. Then the sheets are rolled out over the irrelevancies, the anaesthetist moves in, a screen is adjusted over the face, and, swinging towards the great light, the surgeons hold up their outstretched hands for the final gowning. All eyes bend to the woman; let there be at least a tidy end.

I'm an outsider, a casualty of distracted surprise. At how moved and thrilled I can be at a hand brushing a head. I waive all the further technicalities and tropes of surgery.

Examinations on the Subject of One's Choice

FOR TWENTY-FIVE YEARS I have been having the same nightmare.

I have chosen a field in which I can be preeminent: Classical Greek. At the school-child level. I have already done the final exam, a year ago, and taken the top place and appropriated such glory as belongs to that niche. Now, for reasons never made clear to me, I have decided to take the exam again. Perhaps it is trepidation at the thought of stepping off into a wider world. Perhaps it is the desire to re-run what was a pleasurable, even exhilarating experience. But it is a late decision. I am not even sure that I am still a school-boy. I am hazy about almost everything. I have given away my Goodwin's *Greek Grammar*. I know I have become particularly rusty on the rules for use of the conditional. I hate to think what else might have slipped, but somehow I have to pinpoint these memory losses and then make them good. But Goodwin, and North and Hillard too, are now out of print: the demand, all except mine, seems to have collapsed.

The months, now the days, are stampeding away. The competition this year is stronger than ever: the same faces as before, but a year hungrier, a year's further steady work under their belts. If I looked at no other subject now, read nothing at this stage except the set texts, I would barely get through them – even once. A year ago (or was it only a year – maybe it was two or five or ten?) I knew virtually by heart Plato's *Apology* and *Phaedo*. The examiners have made every concession by putting up the same books; in fact they seem to be making allowances for a lower standard, for they've set a partly translated amalgam of the two, *The Trial and Death of Socrates*. I might still be okay on the narrative and the moments of pathos, but the subtler turns of argument and questions about odd usage would almost certainly throw me. Then the poetry I was never so good at in any case. What's more, I can't seem to find out which play it actually is that I'm to be examined in. Which is it of the grand old men standing at the head of the whole tradition – Sophocles? Euripides? Or have the examiners decided to balance the easy prose with difficult verse, and put on Aeschylus? There's sure to be a question about stichomythia, but the five, or was it six, points I had on it last year just keep eluding me.

It is a matter of days. My energy is draining away in worry and trying to organise myself. I decide to plump for one of the texts – I can't quite see which one – and throw myself into it, but almost immediately there are problems or things I need to look up, and the reference works are nowhere around. I abandon that text, leap into concentrating on another. First make sure of the easy marks here, I tell myself. But they turn out to be not that easy.

There are only minutes to go now. I have left getting to the exam hall too late. I can't find it. There is no notice specifying the location. I've forgotten to fill my pen. I've left my glasses at home. I should have gone to the toilet; I don't know where the nearest one is. The exam will have started by the time I get back. All I can achieve by this venture is humiliation. But I'm here. The clock has struck. The supervisor has said 'You may now commence writing'. I don't know where to start.

'Nothing unusual about any of that,' says my father. 'You can expect to have your nightmare for a lot longer too. In this sort of family, with a bit of get-up-and-go to it, of course you'll have one or two worries about exams.'

'Tell me,' I decide to ask, seeing he's so confidently authoritative – and maybe it's a medical matter as well –'when can I expect it to stop?'

'Failure often does the trick,' he says. 'Maybe your mother has told you how I missed out the first time I went for my primary for the College of Surgeons Fellowship.'

'And you never had the dream again after that?'

'It's like curing the hiccups. You get a good fright and they just stop.'

'But how does it work exactly? And did it cure you?'

'It's when you're convinced you're good at something. The nightmares are the only way any doubts will emerge. Once you've actually had a failure, well, you're more relaxed. You sleep soundly at night. Mind you, I'm talking about one spot of bad luck, not of course about failure in life. That's an entirely different matter.'

I see my father intends to keep his own experience to himself. I'm not sure whether he's even had the nightmare. Once a moral point emerges – and he rather encourages it to do so – it takes hold of him. There's no point in trying to pin him down. You just go elsewhere and start again.

'What other versions of it have there been in the family?'

'Oh, I don't know.' My father doesn't seem inclined to work at the question. 'The old man wouldn't have had too many nightmares, I shouldn't think. I don't know whether he did or not. Not medical ones at any rate. He wasn't that sort of doctor.'

I can detect no note of censure in my father's voice. Yet my usual reading of his views would mean that this has to be a pejorative remark. The sort of doctor who doesn't worry should not be my father's kind of doctor. But perhaps this once he is. Blood has forced my father to be more open-minded in his assessment. Or my reading of him is too doctrinaire.

'The old man's nightmares were more likely to have been to do with the comings and goings of his money. I couldn't tell you much about that. This pacer, or that share in a hotel, or the taxman. The taxman gave him a nasty time once. That must have been as good a nightmare as he had.'

No, I think, I know one better. Very likely my father doesn't know about it. Or he doesn't want to know about it.

'I had a terrible time once,' my grandfather has said to me. 'I half-told your father about it, but he refused to hear evil spoken of the people in question. I dunno what he thought of me in that case. I had to go to the Archbishop to clear my name. But then the Archbishop had half-listened to them in the first place. A nun it was, a sick woman, and her Superior, who should have known better. There's always this bias, you know: they believe any priest or religious before they believe any layman.'

My grandfather remains resolutely oblique on this subject. His exam paper in it, preserved in its manila folder in the Brisbane Archdiocesan Archives, is also an achievement in giving nothing away as much as in denying everything. My father would at least approve of that. If his own father's private letters are, quite wrongfully in his view, to be publicly exposed, then the less they reveal the better. But my father and I say nothing to one another of the letter, nor of the case. Yet it is the nightmare all right.

My grandfather's subject is medicine and the church, his practice of the former among the officials of the latter. Already he has worked at it for over twenty years. His success is obvious to all. His preeminence is widely acknowledged. Then a nun delates him to the Archbishop for unethical conduct. The Archbishop feels him out on the charge. He asks for the Archbishop's wholehearted backing. He does not believe he gets it. He writes demanding full and immediate support.

My grandfather did not preserve papers. The Archdiocesan Archives have no subsequent correspondence in the file. On his deathbed, the Archbishop was attended by my grandfather – as he had been on countless occasions previously. Far from faltering, my grandfather's medical practice among priests, brothers and nuns – unremunerated, as he reminded the Archbishop – never ceased to grow. But it must have lost him plenty of sleep. The danger was patent enough. But there was the hurt there too: the special object of his devotion rearing up against him like that; his most confidently exercised skill being denounced as faulty.

I feel forewarned. What will the real subject be? Surely Classical Greek is merely the emblem of it. As my father's trying to gain fellowship with the surgeons is also only a young man's exercise in showing off his preliminary education.

My father is well aware of this. Good exam results set his warning systems going. 'Life,' he says, 'is the only exam that matters. Ask any old teacher; they'll tell you. It isn't the student who's topped this and that who goes on to the real achievements. It's nearly always someone else. Someone you might hardly have noticed. Your life's the exam,' says my father.

As far as I can see he seems confident of the outcome of his own life. He is resting now, his time is as good as up; he's largely pleased with what he's done, and he's got the opportunity to look over it.

Then the curly one hits him as he's about to leave. He's called to defend his work. His life, it appears, is not going to speak unambiguously for itself. It is alleged he has been negligent. It could be ruinous if he flunks this one. Time is short. He is told the rules. He is told what he can take with him. One of his sons is a doctor, another a lawyer. He is comforted by something complete and satisfying in that. They both advise him. The doctor tells him he is in no condition to go through the ordeal. The lawyer tells him that his upright conscience is blinding him to the whole point of the law. They both say he should come to some accommodation.

That is too easy. He has always been an exacting man. He will not slip flabbily into some meaningless elasticity of words. The worthwhile life is one between narrow lines. Doctor and lawyer should know that. Spotting the erratic is their business. It gives them their preeminence, this concern with the ordained pattern. Each of them, lawyer as well as doctor, holds people trembling in his hand as he turns them this way and that and looks for the flaw.

They speak strongly to him. The lawyer says, 'The fact of the matter is that the law works against the doctor. Like it or not, a jury is inclined to believe the worst of the doctor. Their natural sympathies are with the plaintiff in these matters. Poor bloody patients, they think, helpless victims.'

'My dear boy,' he responds, 'there has been no victim. I did the perfectly correct thing. I have nothing to worry about.'

'That may be so, Dad,' says the doctor, 'but you know better than I that the processes of the law are no light diversion. You're in no fit state to go though all the grilling that's involved.'

'Some sort of settlement is virtually expected in these cases,' says the lawyer. 'Make an offer and get the whole thing cleanly over and done with, and avoid all the aggravation to yourself. You're just not well enough for it. As Guy says.'

'Don't try and tell me about my own health. There has been no fault to be admitted, and the moment I start talking about any settlement – and let's not beat around the bush, compromise is what it would be – the moment I do that, it'll be an admission, or hint, that I made a mistake. I didn't.'

'We all know that,' says the lawyer. 'Settlement is merely a convention of the law. It doesn't imply anything. Nobody's going to start believing you've been professionally at fault.'

'My dear boy, you don't show very much knowledge of human nature.'

The sons roll their eyes at one another. 'You should at least delay it,' says the doctor. 'Till you're a bit stronger.'

'And how much stronger am I likely to get?'

'Look, Dad, let's be honest. If things went badly – you know, if you couldn't handle the questions properly – that'll still be the record that goes to court and there's only one person that will suffer in the long run, and you know who that is.'

He sees red at this. 'Don't you think there's only one consideration in all of this, and that's your mother? Who's to say I won't go off tomorrow with all this business unfinished, and she'd be left burdened with it?'

You won't go off tomorrow, they think. You risk botching it and leaving her an even bigger mess to cope with. You don't give her the credit for the business and administrative skills that would handle some of the ramifications of this better than you ever could. You don't know, you haven't been told – because you are the real innocent that needs protection – that already she's been getting the facts about the worst possible outcome, has been facing up to the moves that might have to be made in that event, knows precisely the sort of money that's being talked about, in brief is methodically doing everything possible to close the opening that your gentlemanly attitude to insurance has left exposed.

But they say nothing. He is impervious to their reason. Medical wisdom probably consists in not harassing him any further.

He takes the law into his own hands. He is less than a month out of hospital. He has lost a long section of his duodenum, one kidney, the use of his rectum, large quantities of necrotic tissue, several gross abnormal fistulas, and numerous of their outcroppings. He has been anointed several times, made a final alteration to his will, and been visited by his sister and brothers coming from interstate to bid him farewell. But he has ridden it out and returned home. Now he is determined to extirpate the sources of this nightmare that bedevilled his drugged dreams in that only just dry-run towards death.

The family dining-room is judged the best place. The full complement of extensions are inserted in the table. Flower bowls are removed, the sideboard cleared of trays and decanters. Upstairs, he dresses and lies on his bed, waiting. They arrive in their respective groups, four silks and their juniors, one for the plaintiff, one for the day's defendant, the others for the cross-plaintiffs embroiled in this. By ten they are all in place, their papers arranged, the stenographer ready. The nod is given, an attendant is sent and the defendant comes downstairs. He is bent at the knees, and his back is curved, and he uses the support the bannister gives. He is informally dressed, a sky-blue jumper and no tie. He turns into the dining-room, and the court, to a man, just manages to restrain the instinctive impulse to rise.

'Good morning, gentlemen,' he says. 'I'm sorry to have put you all to the trouble of coming here.' There is no trace of irony about him. It crosses no one's mind that there might be. Again they repress the instinct to mutter their demurrals.

He sits in his own normal place at the head of the table. Opposite him, at the far end, where the serving is done, in his wife's place, is the controller of this assembly. Between them are the lawyers, their children, taking instructions, full of questions, noting his every word. The figure facing him allots servings, controls the pace, gently corrects, even rebukes, is appealed to in disputes, points to what can be left, what is better chewed on, decides when enough is enough. All the children look to the head of the table, but behind them this mother plays delicately on their reins. The father will lay down for them only as much as she permits.

But this is not a family meal.

You are incompetent, and dangerously so, he is charged.

He rolls with the blow, then weaves forward. No, he thinks, I am leaving bread to the children, not a stone. He opens his arms, and the offering begins to rise and spread out. 'The patient believed he had carcinoma of the lung. He insisted on a complete cycle of tests. He was given them.'

'None of the tests showed any sign of malignancy.'

'The X-rays did.'

'All right, none of the pathology tests.'

'It was the unanimous belief of the chest physicians that this was carcinoma of the lung. But this could be tested only by surgery, and surgery was imperative in any case.'

'You told him what you would do during this surgery?'

'No, that would have been irresponsible, in fact impossible. I have to wait till I am inside before I can see and decide what has to be done.'

'Could you tell us what happened when you opened the chest?'

'There was a tumour in the lower lobe of the left lung. It was obstructing the air passages for both lobes. There was a secondary in the upper lobe. There was already much infection and necrosis and no chance of reversal. The lung was being destroyed. It had to be removed.'

'You removed it before any histo-pathological test was done?'

'Yes.'

'Isn't it normal procedure to have such a test done before removal?'

'No. Not normal. Reasonably common.'

'Is it your normal procedure not to take any histo-pathological specimen when there has been no sign of malignancy before?'

'My normal procedure is to treat every case on its merits. Here I had a heavily infected lung, a tumour, a discrete secondary. The patient could not have long survived with such a diseased organ in him. There was no alternative to removal.'

'But the tumour you removed was not malignant.'

'No, strictly speaking, it was not.'

'Could you tell us what it was.'

'It was some weeks before pathology could give us an answer – an inordinate time to keep a chest wall open. We had to send the specimen around to a number of hospitals and departments before we could get even a tentative answer. You'll hardly find the condition in the text books but I was told it was benign lymphacitic angiitis and granulomatosis.'

'Benign, you say.'

'That is the technical description.'

'So a patient, hearing his condition was benign, could consider himself free from any threat?'

'No. Whatever of the technical term applied, some instances of this condition behave in a malignant way.'

'He has lost a lung, and he hears his condition was benign.'

'His condition was dangerous. Major respiratory problems and large amounts of blood being coughed up. Whereas after his operation he made a rapid recovery. I believe that, against my advice, he went pig-shooting less than a month later.'

'So he does not have a malignant condition, but he is without one lung? His health is impaired?'

'His health subsequent to the operation was considerably better than his health prior to it. His prognosis was what is called guarded.'

'With only one lung, would you agree, it was difficult, in fact impossible, for him to continue practising his profession?'

'With both his lungs in that state it would have been impossible for him to continue living.'

'But you agree his condition was not a carcinoma.'

'Medical terminology would have to be refined. I am led to believe that the patient has recently, more than seven years afterwards, developed secondaries in the other lung and elsewhere in his body. The original excision gave him at least another seven years of life, seven years of grace.'

'I object.'

The paterfamilias does not object. He finds he rather relishes this legal business. He doesn't mind being examined on his life's work. He is more than ever convinced this is not a weak point, but they think it is, and they've brought all their forces to bear on it. It holds.

There is no question of an inquisition, nor of an interrogation. The questioners could not be described as stern. They ask directly and to the point, but their manner is kindly. They are interested only in the law and its strict observance, but the law is all a matter of the treatment of people, and he has no regrets, no bad conscience about his treatment of people. Let them go back to any case and pore over his records. Of course it wouldn't be one triumph after another. There'd be disappointments and failures, a great deal of pain, some passed by in the sheer weight of calls on him, the odd ones affronted by his plain speaking and demands that they help themselves, some utterly unable to respond to the hand he had held out to them. But none of that was damnable. He had made the sick his business, but he didn't fool himself that such a move was itself a short-cut to salvation. The possiblity of forgetting that the object of his profession, the sick, were actually sick was all too easy. He hadn't done that; he'd say it, arrogant though it might be. He was happy to have the questions thrown at him; he was keen in fact. He'd never objected to vivas, and now he'd got a real taste of vivas, not just on his knowledge but on his actions. Where was the examiner?: he was ready for him. Bowl up all the questions on the sick: what he'd done for them, how he'd treated them. He was primed now, itching to present his record. He'd come to the table. They could turn on all the pomp and majesty they liked. They could ask eternally about the sick. He'd jump at the invitation, and he could go on, just as eternally, about the sick and about all his ministrations.

Celestial
Bodies

'OH ALL RIGHT,' she gave in at last.

So later, when they come home from the hospital, he is ready to be compliant. 'Have your bath first. No rush. Just whenever you'd be thinking of going to bed in any case. It'll be best about midnight.'

When she goes upstairs and he hears the water running, he gets into his own pyjamas. Then he pulls his jumper back on, and puts his dressing gown over the top. It is covered in badges. One is that of the Special Air Service Regiment, another says 'Save "Dog of the Week" ', another reads 'Amnesty – Our Voices to Restore Theirs', and yet another, a large white one, says simply 'Australia's Most Interesting Man'. Then he gets out the morning paper again and studies the guide. It tells him that almost everything is starting to move into a negative phase. That the end is in sight. He tears out the long page and carefully folds it over and over so that it becomes a thick wedge he can hold in his hand and that will not flutter nor double up limply. The guide itself sits clear at the top of the wedge.

When he hears the door of the bathroom open, he puts the wedge in his pocket, and sits looking expectantly towards the stairs. He scrutinises her, for just a moment, when she appears. 'Ready?' he asks.

'As long as it doesn't take too long,' she warns him.

He goes to the rack behind the door. 'Here, put Dad's coat on. No, on properly,' he insists. 'It won't be warm enough and it won't stay on just round your shoulders.'

She obeys, and looks at herself, and he lets her laugh first at the bulky coat over the dressing gown over the nightdress. 'Just as well Dad isn't here,' she says. 'I don't think he'd approve.'

'Wait till he hears you've done it.' He makes to correct himself. There is just the slightest twitch of his finger. 'Well, someone'll tell him. Somewhere. I was nearly going to try and tell him when we were leaving. But he wasn't …' He turns and goes into the kitchen, collects a pile of old newspapers and goes out the back door. 'Come on,' he says, and she follows him.

In the middle of the lawn he opens the papers out and spreads them, side by side, on the grass. 'You lie down there, on that side. Make yourself comfortable. I can always put a bit more paper under you if you feel any hard spots.'

'We can be seen, Michael,' she says. 'Whatever will people think? They've just got to walk along the balcony of the units there.'

'Doesn't matter,' he says. 'They'll know what we're doing – if they think about it at all. Come on, we'll both lie down.' He eases himself carefully onto the right side of the paper.

'It'll be damp, Michael,' she says.

'No, it won't. It'll take hours to get through all this paper. Far longer than we'll be here.' He holds up his hand to her. 'Come on, Bubs.'

'I can do it,' she says, brushing him away. She lies down. The movement is brusque but youthful. 'All right,' she says, her arms stiff beside her, 'what do we do now?'

'Just look up and get used to it,' he instructs. He withdraws the guide from his pocket. 'We're looking south,' he begins to intone, and he is both pointing things out to her and finding his own bearings. 'The Southern Cross is slightly to our left. The Pointers are virtually on a level with it. Just keep looking up among the stars. Try to remember not to look at any other lights. Get used to the dark.'

They are both silent for a moment, concentrating. Under them the mat of newspaper crackles. It tunes itself for the exertion. It tenses itself and falls still.

'Okay,' he says, raising his left hand. 'Up we go.' His fingers trace a tentative, bobbing path across the sky. 'Into the perihelion.'

'What are you doing?' she asks.

'Finding my way past Omega Centauri.'

'Stop showing off.'

'Hang on,' he says. 'Don't distract me.' He glances at the guide, then at the sky ahead, then back again. 'Must be to the left.' His arm jerks.

'Careful,' she calls. 'Don't bump.'

'The faster he goes the better we'll see him. But he dodges here and there, lets the other bodies obscure him. Stick close.'

People traverse the walkways around them, peer when they catch a glimpse of the mat and its supine explorers.

'Look at them, Michael,' she calls, 'they're staring.'

'Don't worry,' he shouts, 'we're miles away.'

She sets her face firmly ahead, her mild frown braving the darkness, seizing on the distant, uncertain lights. 'You sure we'll see him,' she asks, 'in all this? I don't recognise anything.'

'You'll see him. He's behind the sun, but the sun illuminates him.'

'Don't go too near the sun.'

'No worry. He won't hurt us. Just keep your eyes skinned for the old comet.' He cups his hands to form blinkers round his eyes, and he peers intently. 'Maybe we should go further up,' he says, and glances at his watch. 'Yes, it's just about on midnight. Up, up,' he encourages, 'towards the zenith. Hang on.'

She leans slightly in towards him, to lay her eyes upon his line of vision. 'What will we see?'

'Light,' he says.

'So clear we can't miss it?'

'Probably not.'

'Spectacular or just steady?'

'Should be both, but it'll probably be quiet, understated. Look for the tail. A spread of light fanning out from the sharp centre.'

She wraps her arms over her chest in concentration, pulling the collars of the overcoat upright against her neck. They race further and further into space, and together their eyes scour the firmament.

The rustling of the newspaper is lost in the hum of the cavernous world.

'Look,' she cries. 'There! Is that it?' She plucks him by the arm.

'Could be. Could be. Where exactly?'

'There, there. On top of the Cross.'

He looks. 'Yes,' he cries. He holds the guide out in front of him again, and takes bearings. 'You're right. That's him.'

The tension relaxes, and they glide. Soundlessly they take in the comet. It glitters smokily before them. The sparks irradiate around it. The power of it hangs heavy in the galaxy.

'He's almost resting,' she says, 'priming himself for something new.'

'He's on his way out. Gearing up to go back into the darkness.'

'But he doesn't look finished. Not with all that puff.' She laughs.

Their vast amphitheatre purrs.

'He's probably in good condition. Leviathan,' she says.

'Beg pardon?'

'Isn't that the word?'

'Why not?'

The great static projectile bathes them in its light. They hover and sideslip around it while their mat moves and creaks in the tug and slack of the breeze. Their shadows run wild as the comet shows now its face, now its underside, and its great fan of sparks sags and rears. It surrounds them, the unique grandeur of it confronting them whichever way they move.

'Remarkable,' she says. 'That we live in such a shadow. Who'd ever have guessed it.'

'True,' he says. 'It's only when you see it going.'

They watch the comet revolve.

'It won't be long now,' he says. 'A matter of days. So the professionals say.'

She leans forward. 'Yes, he does seem to be slowing down. We should watch him till he goes.'

The brightness of the tail rises and falls. Brilliance follows dullness and recedes again. But not regularly. The movement is spasmodic.

'I could believe,' she says, 'that he is panting.' She touches her son on the arm. 'Stay with me, while I stay with him.'

He holds the mat steady, and noiselessly irons away the rustles and the crackling. Then he anchors them by the head of the comet. Without a sound mother and son adjust their positions and settle in. Their consciousness is attuned only to the transient comet. They say nothing, they breathe with him, they look at him without once turning their eyes away. They see the darkness coming up, rolling in, small waves at first. Their eyes follow him as he meets it, the first clouds moving over him but merely blurring him at the edges. He comes out the other side, and he is sharp and whole again, but a new billow swirls in and he goes under for a moment and is lost to sight. He reappears, but less distinctly, and they hold their own breaths waiting for the exhalation to lighten up the sky. It comes, and again comes, but the intervals are ever more protracted, and the darkness builds its strength with every blow it delivers until it blots out and smothers the whole comet and its minutest spark.

For a time they do not move. But under them the newspaper begins to crackle again. A current of air catches it and turns up the edges and they flap.

'That's it, Bubs,' he says, and he jumps up. He stretches, beats his chest with both fists, and pulls the dressing gown and the badges on it tighter.

'Here, Michael, give me a hand,' she says. 'Don't you get stiff?'

He turns round and grasps both her hands and yanks her to her feet. She pretends to lose her balance and cries out, half in laughter.

'Quiet,' he teases her as he gathers the paper. 'You'll wake all the neighbours.'

She laughs again. 'Imagine me doing that.'

'Come on, Bubs,' he says. He slips his arm through hers and together they go up the stairs to bed.

A
Definition
of
Happiness

AS A CHILD I was taught to pray for a happy death. Not obsessively, not publicly, not even overtly. But the formulas were there, and I came across them, naturally, like the country child learning about sex. It was not that they were put in my way, nor that I was simply allowed to see them. The noticing, the reading, the recitation of them were inseparable from all the other advances of childhood. My mother was primarily responsible. But, again, only in the unmeditated way in which a parent finds herself accompanied by the child around the various storehouses and treasuries that provision and enrich her life.

She had a missal, dating from her boarding school days, wondrous enough itself for all the arcane and unintelligible matter that it contained – prayers in time of pestilence, prayers for the churching of women, prayers for the conversion of Mary's dower. But interleaved throughout the book was a multitude of mementos of my mother's spiritual history. The phrase is too grandiloquent of course. It would normally suggest notes or other indications of a soul's progress. There would almost be anger in my mother's laugh at the absurdity of such a phrase being applied to her. But what is interleaved documents the appearance of this friend, the disappearance of this relation, the elevation of this acquaintance, and thereby the addition of a particular prayer to the repertoire that my mother would regularly work her way through.

Here is a holy picture given her by a Dominican nun. Her patron saint, Blessed Imelda, so young but dying, is miraculously receiving the Host in the midst of her religious sisters. I sit beside my mother on the bench during Mass, and if she exchanges the missal for her rosary or puts it down to go to Communion, I stare at the picture and try to work out the story of Blessed Imelda, and turn to the back for guidance, but it contains only a prayer – for her canonisation, for acceptance of God's will, for a happy death. I want details of a life, a personality; I want something individual, and I get merely a formula, a prayer. I'm conscious of disappointment, I'm aware of feeling flat. After all the suggestiveness of a picture, the reverse side of the card is colourless, even bloodless. But I read through it, cursorily enough, and my imagination begins to agitate to be let out past the dreariness of it to play somewhere.

There are my mother's mortuary cards. They are all of men, the mortal sex. The uncle-in-law who gave her away at her wedding, the brother-in-law lost in action three months before that wedding. The dead are pictured, not in some washed-out reproduction in the card, but in tipped-in photographs, miniatures of the face, cut not quite squarely, as though they were cut out and assembled by my mother herself and gathered into her album of the family saints, to be greeted at least every Sunday in all their two-dimensional immediacy, and prayed with and prayed for in the long run-up to their resurrection, and hers, and all the family's.

My mother says hello to them matter-of-factly. She is reverent, but not piously or ostentatiously so. She works through the prayers, turns the faces away, back into the long Latin columns of never-ending inspiration and petition. She lays the black cross on the reverse of the card down again on the dead. The wish and the prayer for a happy death hover among the other formal and altruistic cries. She does not need to dwell on it. The formula on the mortuary cards is merely a gloss. The primary text is a phrase in the Hail Mary. She would use it at least ten times every day. Pray for us, my mother asks the Virgin, at the hour of our death. As the Virgin prayed, presumably successfully, at Christ's death. But where is the happiness in that? Who is to say that the faces on the mortuary cards were smiling at their moment? Both of them taken suddenly and violently, one attacked from within his own organism, the other probably struck down by another human being. Yet who knows the last emotion at the centre of any soul?

There is a metaphysical cheek about the whole notion of a happy death. But I was used to it as the most mundane and reasonable of requests. You do not keep asking for something, day after day, generation after generation, unless it is as normal an object of obtainable desire as one's daily bread, or forgiveness, or safety from harm. Perhaps, in itself, a happy death could be a perfectly secular notion, but it sits well as a Christian paradox. Money is of no value, I'm told. Flesh and blood are sacred, I'm told, but equally a man's enemies shall be those of his own house. These are the truths of the world. A happy death is no wierder a notion. So you live cheerfully with the dead.

'What about your father?' I say to my mother. 'Where's his card?'

The lack doesn't worry her. It hasn't occurred to her as such. He has been dead since before she was three. Three-year-olds aren't given mortuary cards of their own. As far as I, a child, can tell, his death is not one that impinges on her. He isn't listed, least of all in pride of place at the beginning, in the litany of the dead that concludes our family prayers. Increasingly I feel guilty about this. In comparison to a mother's father the others on our list seem interlopers.

'Daddy?' asks my mother when he is yanked into her presence like this. The word seems alien in her mouth. There are perhaps two sentences in which she uses it: 'Daddy took that photograph' of his wife-to-be and all her siblings and parents; and 'I must clean up Daddy's plate', meaning the brass fixture which has lain for decades, dulling, under the house. I cannot guess what meaning the word has for her, what sensation she experiences when the tongue clatters over the palate with it. Did she ever use it in the second person? For probably about a year. But not as a small child to the strong one, the comforter, the everlasting prince. Daddy was a figure on a bed, not one who raised the child from hers. Daddy meant a consumptive wreck, waning as she waxed. What memory did she have of even that, in any case, what familiarity with that particular sound going crying from her mouth?

So the term was reserved almost exclusively for the father of her own children, and it was still a third-person usage. A vocative use, natural and familial if a little cloying, did not come easily to her. She doesn't throw the term 'Daddy' around in any carefree way. Daddies are creatures that die.

This one is in hospital, for the fifth time in fewer years. There is to be no surgery this time. She has heard the story and nodded. In the first stages of the attack the invaders come on singly. They are hacked, chopped, despatched as each appears and is discovered. So they emerge in pairs, then in further multiples, and concert their rushes. The warrior has too few hands to cut them down, and, besides, he has become exhausted. He is tied to his pillar and simply made comfortable there. He is rushed, and overrun, nothing can be done.

So, is this a happy death? I watch her, on guard over the ruins. Oh it's dignified enough, but who is interested in that. A dignified death is a pinched notion, a threadbare secular consolation. A happy death is an infinitely bolder idea. But can we call it that? Can she? The doses of morphine are increased, the heart races, the lungs cannot keep pace, oxygen and blood can no longer keep their proper distance, and he is smothered. Or the dead tissue comes away, and whirls along the stream until it catches and clots, then breaks free again and races into the lung and catches and is lodged there irremovably, and he suffocates. Certainly not easy or untroubled deaths, either of them.

He has owned up to discomfort – great, terrible discomfort – but hardly to anything more. Discomfort is the great medical euphemism, but if it is the appropriate word for others in their distress, he won't try to go beyond it for himself either. Yet such carnage among the blood cells, so much excision and rerouting among the organs, so much necrosis of the tissue, all rage that their effect can be described as mere discomfort. Yet maybe he knows that the boundary between discomfort and pain is fuzzy, even intangible, and being ascetic but gentle he has always veered towards a conservative position. Discomfort passes over into pain when … it hardly matters. You try to relieve one as much as the other.

'Tell him about Carol Winterbottom's phone call,' says one of the sons.

Sitting beside him, both hands holding one of his, she leans back, looks over and gives them a smile that says 'You're bold, but I'm tempted.'

'Yes, do, he'd like that,' says another son.

She leans into his ear again, and her fingers tap against the back of his hand. 'Carol Winterbottom rang last night,' she enunciates. 'She wanted to speak to you.'

He grimaces. Just slightly. His eyes are closed, but a tremor passes across his face. If he is actually reacting to her, the expression may in fact be pained, but it is more likely to be histrionic horror.

He has always taken amused pride in his miniscule private, and honorary, general practice. The mothers of priest friends, former patients of his father who have moved from Brisbane to Sydney, nuns who have taught his wife. Carol is the second wife of Tommy, an old Queenslander and a hard-drinking man. Occasionally she cannot do anything with him, and she calls in the cardiac surgeon. She's at her wits' end. The cardiac surgeon has the authority and knowledge. But this time Tommy is constipated. Grossly so. Embarrassment is a minor inconvenience of the distant past. The condition has been with him for weeks. He is on his bed groaning. 'Newspaper, Carol,' says the cardiac surgeon, 'and your kitchen gloves, and a basin of warm water.'

'There's no other way to deal with impacted faeces,' he says. 'You've just got to get your hand in, and dislodge them, bit by bit. Once you get the plug out, you're okay to try other things. But it's that rock-like mass gumming things up at the end that's the problem. Fingers are the only thing for it.'

Tommy is a great big heavy man. There is lots of pushing and rolling and rolled-up shirtsleeves work. Later, for years later, there is lots of laughter over this story. The cardiac surgeon tries to restrain his own mirth to an ethical chuckle. It's not easy, and he distracts himself by drawing the ethical moral. He gets very righteous very quickly. He has a feeling that soiling the hands might do some of his own children a bit of good. 'If you won't do that, I don't care how good you are at anything else. If I had a resident or a registrar and he showed the slightest hesitation when it came to a job like that, he was no good to me. I don't care how many

University Medals he's got, or how brilliant his other reports were, if he showed a skerrick of distaste at relieving someone with impacted faeces, then as far as I was concerned he was out. If you're unwilling to relieve a patient's distress – and I don't care how dirty or ignoble the work is – then you shouldn't be in medicine.'

The pupils, the colleagues, those who have studied and trained under him, slip quietly in the door. They say nothing, they do not disturb the family. They stand at the foot of the bed and look at the dying man. Several, the older ones, those nearer to him in age, slip to the head of the bed and tap his hand while they lean down and kiss him on the forehead. One stands at the foot a little unsurely, then tweaks the toes through the coverlet. All spend some moments almost at attention at the feet. You can hear and see the salute, the farewell to the chief. The family don't move, they hardly seem to advert to this procession of the junior commanders, but they allow room for the other life, the one that was not theirs. His wife nods and gives a proxy acknowledgement of each salute.

She grasps him by the hand. 'Carol Winterbottom rang to say she was rewriting her will. She wants to leave something to you.' Around the bed they all laugh over again at the joke. Carol Winterbottom's timing is not a cruel irony. It is simply a good joke to be relished. It is appropriate in every way. He deserves well at the hands of the Winterbottoms. But equally, after a lifetime of imperviousness to commercial enterprise or speculation, he should not now be reaping any sort of financial harvest.

At the other side, one of his sons leans down and repeats it. 'Did you hear that, Dad? Carol Winterbottom wants to leave you her money. Squeeze Ma's hand if you can hear.'

He enjoys being tantalised by the notion that you get your reward in this life. He enjoys seeing the reward come close, knowing that it will swerve again at the last moment. He is no longer subject to any hormonal rush of desire, or to the elation that rises from a sudden expansion of material possibilities. His smile reflects a purely spiritual or at least intellectual pleasure. He knows how ultimately impotent the strongest temptations are against him. He is relishing the pointed moral – for those of his pupils and successors who have fallen from grace into money and fastidiousness – that soiling yourself in the pre-scientific, merely comforting care of the sick might, laughably, be the most lucrative form of medical practice.

Even subtler morals ripple over his clear, still mind. Grubbing out the handfuls of Tommy's impacted faeces he sees that even as he's withdrawing them they turn, as in all the miracles and fairytales, into fistfuls of dollars. But then, even as his hand is recoiling under the crackle of this new, foreign touch, the dollars disintegrate and the dust finds nowhere to lodge and slides away down between his fingers. He's left holding nothing, but his hands are surgically clean, and Tommy is sighing and swearing gently with pleasure. 'Fucking Mother of God,' says Tommy, 'that's better.'

A smile trembles across the face of the dying man. Everyone agrees it does.

'Will you say the rosary with us, Dad,' she whispers, and they all kneel down. The five Sorrowful Mysteries, she announces. It's not a lugubrious, tactless choice for the dying. She remembers a rare statement of spiritual disposition: 'I've always preferred the Sorrowful Mysteries,' he had said. 'They're the only ones that mean anything to me.' Not being a melancholy man, this avowal might have appeared uncharacteristic of him. Cheerful, even-tempered, and utterly uncomprehending of such experiences as angst, he is not a likely candidate for meditating on scourgings and crownings with thorns. But of course he belongs to an empirical tradition. His taste is for the tangible, not the speculative or the imaginary. He is after all a surgeon, not a physician, much less a psychiatrist. Crownings in heaven are a future he never doubts, but it is only a formal, notional assent he gives to them. Pain is what he can put his finger on and feel. It is a nice thought that such is the aspect of Christianity his spirit is at home in. Compensations and rewards and glittering prizes leave him unmoved. But suffering is what he knows, and if religion presents it to him as a central object of meditation, that makes sense to him, and he'll go along with it.

His breathing becomes more stertorous. The air runs into membranes of blood and mucus in the throat, and spins around noisily looking for an exit. Tubes are inserted and the air passages are vacuumed. His sons sponge his mouth and wipe away the detritus building up on his teeth and his tongue. But below, in the trunk and out in the limbs, the body is disintegrating. Rags of tissue come away and surge along the race of blood, bobbing and colliding with other casualties of erosion and devastation, all converging, intent on suffocation, on the brain. Sucking and sponging only palliate momentarily; they have to be applied more and more frequently; there is hardly a break in their work on the drowning man, and then they are withdrawn, useless.

The Sorrowful Mysteries are traversed. His face strains under the weight of them. She can do nothing more to ensure his happiness. She hopes maybe that he can be distracted, that some incidental on the road ahead can take his mind off the passion of it. Carol Winterbottom's will? Tommy long dead, but all his savings coming to Harry at this stage. His children are kissing his forehead and skull and giving him messages, but maybe his mind is somewhere else. As so often. Puzzling, worrying over one of his cases. But smiling to himself too, one of his private jokes. Tommy Winterbottom's bountiful cache.

A
Problem
of
Wardrobe

THE SHROUD SITS in the bottom drawer, with the scarf and the gloves and the Aran jumper – all the items that Sydney does not call for. Only when I go away do they come out.

My father's sister came to the presumed deathbed. She took me aside, away from my mother's hearing. 'I rang the Carmelites and asked for prayers before I came away. They asked me would I like the shroud, you know … the habit to bring down for Harry. Dad was buried in one. I didn't know whether you'd want that too. I'll leave it with you.'

My father pulled through. I took the shroud home, without mentioning, without showing it to anybody. It was compact and wrapped in butcher's paper. I saw no need, felt no wish to open it. I put it where it would be out of the way but reachable. I did not want its flat permanence spoiling the lively rhythm of the constantly shrinking, constantly growing piles of T shirts and underpants. I put it down with my items of traveller's wardrobe, and opened a new packet of camphor on it.

A year later my father dies. My mother gives orders, ten minutes after the last breath, that his best, his newest suit be brought to the hospital, as well as the red tie she had bought him at Hunt's for Christmas and the shirt that would be found in its cellophane wrapper on the left hand of the top drawer of his wardrobe. As she leaves the room to detail these orders I decide I had better make my running.

I have no interest in the matter; it is merely a duty that has been laid on me. Whatever the case with his own father, I feel the religious habit is totally wrong for mine. But self-interest may appear to be present: I am conscious that once in the past I retrieved two suits of my father's from the Vincent de Paul bag and had them modified cheaply and minimally to be a perfect fit for me.

The occasion shouldn't even admit this pondering of factors. My mind should be washed clean, merely going through routines on automatic. But I find no such purity. I would keenly like the chance for a prologue or an explanation for my offer. I'm not sure I can trust I have a reputation for commonsense and unselfishness. Or even taste and decorum. Not even with my own mother. But the occasion makes no allowances for self-preservation.

'Half a sec.' I pluck my mother by the sleeve as she moves out into the corridor. I try to make it a private word with her. 'I'm not recommending it, but the Carmelites have sent down a ... habit, if you'd like to use it.'

She only half turns to me, but she looks keenly into my eyes, and then is already facing away from me again before she speaks. 'No, certainly not,' she says. There has been no pause, and she is downright decisive, almost peremptory. I have never seen it before. I back off, shrugging. This is her death, not mine. My head shakes in little more than a shiver, and my tongue and my breath take themselves for a dry run through the word no, and my hands revolve through quarter circles of deprecation.

I am left with the shroud.

I could send it back. I could send it back to my aunt in Brisbane, but that would be to imply that it is no use to me, and that she or one of her brothers or one of the family up there will be the next to have a use for it, and that would be an indelicate gesture.

I could send it back to the Carmelites, but that would smack of the churlish and the ungracious. Besides, I have had it now for two years. Gifts are not returned after that length of time.

I could throw it out. But it is a perfectly good garment, unused, pristine: I have no capacity for that sort of wastefulness.

Then I could give it to a good cause, to Vincent de Paul. But V de P is made up of good, down-to-earth people who don't want this sort of fancy dress clogging up their distribution of essentials. They'd suspect it of being a costume for the Gay Mardi Gras or the work of some pious zealot who thinks she'll do some good for religion by making this sort of apparel available. Either way it wouldn't be beyond them to trace the donor, and I'd prefer not that.

The possibilities become less and less feasible. Turning it into, say, some kind of pass-the-parcel joke among relatives and close friends. That would be demeaning: flippant use of an object accepted with, and intended for, some solemnity. On the other hand, it is the sort of family that could take on board such a joke and not be coarsened by it – once the joke were properly launched. But I'm not sure that I could do that.

In any case, such concerns only make sense if I'm determined to unload the thing at all costs. I'm not. I've been left with it, but that need not be heard as a statement of put-upon, resigned passivity. I'm left with it. I'm not upset at that.

The shroud is, more accurately, a religious habit, but one tailored for specific and sole use as a shroud. It sits in the drawer beside the bed. As I lie beside my wife I can see the handle that will draw it out. Now that it is there, I remember that elsewhere in the house, located somewhere in what I call my archives, are other badges of the dedicated religious life. Somewhere between letters from old girlfriends and comic verse circa 1965 is a small chain of fine wire that can be clipped over the calf or the thigh or the upper arm so that the ingrown points of each link can press, without quite puncturing, into the surface of the skin. And beside it is tucked a small discipline of thin but superior-quality rope, with six tails, each issuing in a resin-hardened knot, delicately tuned to go almost, but never quite, to the point of drawing blood.

What are they doing there? I take it for granted that I will not be using them again. I would regard it as cheap and contemptible to produce them for a party trick. I am not a hoarder of the merely curious, I have no difficulty in throwing away, I am not a constant envisager of what might come in handy. Now that I have the shroud, I like the sense of their presence there. I don't want anything more. What there is has spontaneously supervened. Actively to go and complete the wardrobe – after all a skull is the only thing that is lacking (I grew up with a skull: everyone in a medical household does) – is repugnant, pointless, and a camp affectation, and it only occurs to me as a possible course of action when I reflect upon the oddity of these possessions.

I don't draw attention to the presence of the shroud, the chain and the discipline. My wife is unaware of their existence here. I see no reason to tell her. I know wives of former colleagues of mine who deeply resent the years of idealistic and comradely foolishness – or was it foolhardiness – in which they had no part. My wife is not like that. In her moments of blackest bitterness, so fierce that it interferes even with her accuracy, she gladly yields me up. 'You're so totally self-centred,' she says. 'You should never have left the priesthood.'

As far as possible clothing should be hung. That is the axiom. When clothing is packed away it is only for the season. It is folded and put in cupboards, drawers, suitcases merely so that it will be out of the way, so that it won't confuse and hamper the choice of wear at times when its use would be totally inappropriate.

But clothing is hung, paradoxically, when its use is likely to be either immediate or so far into the future as to seem unlikely. Private households rarely have the articles belonging to this second category in their wardrobes. But they are found, hung or worn by mannequins, in museums, palaces, theatre warehouses. When neither situation obtains, textile curators, I believe, advise that as far as possible fabrics should be stored flat and unfolded. The same principles apply to cloth as to paper or vegetable matter or skin: a flat, ironed-out position is best if one is to avoid wrinkles and the consequent drying-out, darker lines and eventual friability of those creased sections. If flat planes are not the nature of the article, it is still best to hang it in such a way that the drapery finds its own natural sags, folds and contours. The article will enjoy longer life if allowed an environment of relaxed space, subdued light, air movement and of course freedom from vermin.

But I can't hang the shroud up. The arguments are overwhelming. Its presence best remains a secret. Even were the secret to come out, it has been my personal choice to live with the article, but there should be no thrusting of the object into the daily vision of other people. My wife riffles through her dresses, making the choice for some sweetly anticipated evening, and her fingers slide across into my section of the wardrobe and brush the stiff, harsh, dun-brown cloth. Not fair. Or she fights for space for what is immediately wearable and practical, and tries to eliminate what doesn't fit, or is unfashionable, and she has to contend with this thing. Like a dog, the poor creature becomes an object of annoyance, even loathing – and it is all the doing of the master, the owner. For its own good, to save it from inevitable maltreatment, I have to be cruel to be kind, and keep it in a dark place, unable to be mentioned, gradually going stiff and brittle, taking unnatural shapes, gathering an un-wholesome complexion.

Once I had various items in my drawers, my trunks, on my bookshelves, that I preferred other people did not see. There is little now that I find has to be kept hidden. My domain is encroached upon, shared, no longer thought of as particularly mine. The bottom shelf of the bedroom bookcase I kept fairly empty. That saved bending; it hoisted the books above the lazier, floor-bound cockroaches and silverfish; it could be used as a temporary deposit for transient newspapers and magazines.

Its very availability was my nemesis. Now it is stuffed with volumes of adventure, a teeming jostle of bears, dingos, pirates, dogs, grenadier guards, dinosaurs, vehicles, frogs, all embroiled in a massive welter of confusion and discovery. Their friend and leader essays out with them from the shelf and across the floor, and is sometimes lost, sometimes chalks up another new world, sometimes settles further into old habits of belief, obduracy and rhetoric. There's no holding back the tide of his advances and retreats. But beyond the bookcase, past the clothes horse, beside the mirror is my clothes chest, and I have seen the boy abandon princesses and pink panthers and come to the bottom drawer, and place his fingers on the brass handles, and turn and look at me.

'Don't go near that drawer, Harry,' I shout at him. 'That's Daddy's.'

Legacies

HALF AN HOUR before the start of the Rugby Test my mother has all her sons together. 'While I've got you here,' she says, 'would you come upstairs. It won't take long.'

She leads us into her bedroom. On the expanse of the well-made bed she has laid my father's clothes and personal effects. On one side are draped the shirts, all on hangers, all freshly ironed. Jumpers, singlets, shorts, underpants, are in their separate piles, all folded. The ties, doubled-over once, lie across the bed in a narrow fan. There is a bobbing fleet of boxes for cuff-links, shirt studs, even tie pins. Belts cluster in the middle, wound into relaxed reels. There is not really very much. The suits have been left in the wardrobe. There are only three of them. The best one went with him.

I stand at the foot of the bed. Beside me Michael curls his arm around the corkscrewed post and rests his foot on the cross-beam. Hugh looks serious beside my father's pillow. John stands to my right, indecisive between solemnity and his more natural comradeliness. Guy hovers somewhere, not quite in sight.

My mother positions herself between the bedside table and the wardrobe. 'Well, go on,' she says. 'You're to take whatever you want.' And she gives a jerk of her wrist, a gesture of slight impatience.

It crosses my mind that if I were running this event, I would make it a bit more orderly. By having us all take turns in selecting items. But we're obedient, and we all move in, hands feinting a little, solicitous to avoid falling where another hand has landed.

'Don't hold back,' says my mother, emphasising the point with another of her gestures. It could be argued she is inciting, but she has a confidence in her sons she is not even conscious of. And in fact the hands, fluttering and tentative in those first moments, all land with precision, apart.

I go first to the jumpers. They are not nearest. Perhaps they are most identifiably my father. No, they just rather appeal to me. My mother has had elbow patches put on in the last six months. I have never had a sky-blue jumper, and I would just like to have this article, for its own sake. When I take the jumper home, my wife will say, 'Just wear it for around the house. For a while. Your mother would be upset seeing you in it. It's so much your father over those last six months.' But I also reach for the jumpers because I know they are too small for anyone else. Practicalities and tastes assert themselves spontaneously.

Michael has to wear suits every day. He takes first inspection of the shirts and ties. Guy takes medical items. Or, rather, they are picked out for him: College of Surgeons tie, St Vincent's cuff-links. The trousers are hardly touched; they are too short for anybody but me, but they have eight inches more in the waist than I need. My mother watches, encourages, and suggests. 'Which of you wear singlets?' she asks. We all protest loudly, laughingly, that we do. She believes – or, rather, we pretend she believes – that wearing singlets is next to godliness. But these singlets are sleeved cotton in summer mesh. We all murmur that we don't wear that sort. She gets no takers. 'All right: St Vincent de Paul,' she says, decisively but without any rancour.

I turn to the cuff-link boxes. Hugh has been through them already. I note that he has taken the pair I always used when I had to wear cuff-links and automatically borrowed them from my father.

But an airline captain has more cause for elegant wrists than I do. I go through the other boxes, surprised how many there are. The taste is dreadful; monograms and flashiness and overstatement. 'I didn't realise he had so many of these,' I say, mildly and generally to my mother.

'Presents,' says Guy. 'Hospitals and the like are always giving those sorts of presents. Ugly aren't they?'

'Hideous,' I say.

'Just what V de P wants,' says Michael.

My mother isn't really listening to facetiousness. 'I know somewhere for them,' she says.

'You shouldn't just give away presents like that,' says Hugh, 'especially when they're engraved.'

'True,' I say. 'It's a problem.' But not mine.

'Give me that, Hugh,' my mother is saying. 'I'll use it for dusters.'

'You certainly won't,' he says. 'This is an antique. Nineteen thirty ... when was it?' He is holding up a football jumper, now barely more than off-white, with only smudges of its former sky-blue, but with a still vivid waratah sewn to the left breast.

'It's an attractive jumper, the New South Wales one,' I say. 'Restrained.'

'If no one else wants it,' says Hugh, 'I'll take it.'

'You played less football than anyone, Hugh,' says my mother.

'Well, I'm very suitable then. He only ever played one game in this jumper.'

'Only because he was too light,' says Guy, quoting someone. 'A lovely centre, a beautiful player, but just too light. Watch out for the moths on it,' he says to Hugh.

Hugh, the youngest, takes the oldest item there.

John has found the reefer jacket in the wardrobe. He pulls it on, and he does have to pull too. The left cuff has drawn clear of his watchband. He flexes his shoulders back, then hunches forward again, and goes up to the mirror on my mother's dressing table. 'What do you think?' he says. What we think is that he's doing a Cinderella's sister trying on the glass slipper. Except that his face registers nothing nastier than hope and the first creakings of resignation.

Guy makes it easy for him. 'Not really, Johnno,' he says. He is smiling, but not grinning. The rest of us make sure we don't catch

John's eye, not just at that moment, the instant of disappointment. John takes one last look in the mirror, grunts softly, then the coat is off and he's forgotten it. I'm three inches shorter than any of the others: the coat is mine or nobody's. I riffle through the hankies, although it's twenty years since I've used hankies. Then I turn, as though absently, and pick up the jacket, as though by chance. It fits perfectly.

'Just right,' says Guy. He seems to be observing and guiding the rest of us rather than attending to himself.

'T'rrific,' says Michael.

I'm tempted to leave it on. But I lay it on the floor on the top of my pile.

'What about all these other things?' says my mother. She is determined on the maximun turnover. 'These are perfectly good pyjamas.'

None of us denies that. But none of us, it appears, has much use for summer pyjamas.

Only oddments seem to be left, miscellaneous items. We are reluctant to walk away too quickly, loath to show any of the features of marauders or scavengers. 'Nothing else here you want?' my mother probes. Nestling against her own pillow are various boxes and containers, garage sale sort of stuff. But Hugh, with the confidence of the youngest, walks round and picks up a half-hidden wooden box. I have not seen it since I was a child. It is of inlaid wood, probably only pine, but perfectly finished and with a large stylised kangaroo, also in inlay, on the lid. There are delicate suggestions of Aboriginal style and motif about the object, but it is neither mere imitation nor pastiche. It is subdued, classical, quite the reverse of kitsch. It is an oddity in this unnationalistic household. Hugh does not waste time over the box itself. He opens it with a casual spontaneity I am barred from.

'Dad's medals,' he says, holding them out across the palm of his hand. It is the full ceremonial set, circles of metal dependent from their bars of ribbon. I don't think I have ever seen them. Never having had an ostentatious owner, they are impressive. I know they are only service medals, general issue, not the spectacular stars or crosses of officially recognised unusual conduct. But they are the testament to lost years, to his enforced turning back after setting his hand to the plough of a vocation.

'Gerry can wear these now,' says Hugh. 'The eldest son in the place of his father.'

'Put them back,' says my mother. 'I'll keep them.' It is impossible to gauge her tone. But it is not rebuke nor thwarting. If it is for reasons to do with herself, they are invisible. It may well be to save me from embarrassment, even from a possible ridiculousness. A mother protecting her child from his dubious paternal inheritance. But that may be quite fanciful. She gives nothing away.

To cover any awkwardness for either of us I sift my hand through the other items beside the kangaroo box. I encounter smoothly indented, concave metal. It is a hip flask. I lift it up. The concavity of it is sensual. Broad-shouldered but refined, smooth, flowing away inwards in its diastole, and then curving back again in its perfect systole.

'Could I have this?' I ask.

'The hip flask?' says my mother. 'You don't drink.'

'Neither did Dad really, if it comes to that,' I counter.

'Well ...' chorus the other boys, the unmarried ones, who knew more of his daily habits over the last few years.

I unscrew the top and sniff. 'This, at any rate, hardly seems to have been used.'

'Of course you can take it if you want it,' says my mother.

I move my fingers backwards and forwards over the slim surface of it. Any other function for the object seems beside the point. It's not really for a hip; the name must be a euphemism. It's not for me to carry emergency alcohol in either. It must be cheap, it must be one of millions; it will have no use, but it is beautiful.

'That's his Sam Browne,' my mother is saying.

Michael is holding up a broad, ungainly length of dull brown leather. He is looking at it in puzzlement.

'Don't you know what a Sam Browne is, Michael?' says my mother.

'Issue to all officers,' says Hugh.

'Who was Sam Browne?' asks Michael.

No one knows. I say I'll look it up.

'They look all right when they're on,' says Hugh. 'On properly.'

'Go on, Mike,' says Guy. 'No one else wants it.'

'We'll draw straws,' says Michael.

'Keep it,' we all shout at him. 'No one else wants it.'

'Right,' he shouts back, 'but we're drawing straws for these.' He holds up a large white cardboard box. 'Just you and me and Hugh. John and Guy have got theirs.' He slips out the flap on the lid, reaches in and pulls out by its strap the large black case for what must be a pair of binoculars.

'Judge Herron's present,' murmurs my mother. She seems to have forgotten these. She's not objecting to their going, but she doesn't seem to have actually put them out either.

I'm bewildered. I know nothing of Judge Herron or his present. Except that, however generous it might have been, it was also hopelessly inappropriate. My father wanted nothing more than his naked eyes on his walks, and he may have blundered onto a racecourse by mistake twice in his life.

'Eldest goes first,' cries Michael. He holds his closed fist out to me, three small sticks just peeping over the knuckle of his index finger.

'Hang on,' I call. 'What's the rule? Biggest or smallest straw wins?'

Hugh lounges in the background, his half-smile on his face, apparently detached.

'Smallest wins.'

'Okay.' I feint towards the middle straw, veer to the left, then jerk back to my first choice – what so obviously shouldn't be the one to pick. I slide it out. I have no idea whether it's short or long.

'Bugger,' shouts Michael, and swinges down with his left hand. 'No more goes needed.' He dances around in mock rage.

'I take it that's the short one,' I say.

'Course it's the short one,' he yells at me. Hugh laughs.

'Blowed if I know what I'm going to do with them,' I say. 'I probably should have disqualified myself.'

'Too late,' shouts Michael. 'As long as you give us goes.'

'Yes, of course. If anyone's going to the races or for a hike or anything, just let me know. Maybe we can rotate them.'

'They're yours,' says Michael, and he thrusts them against my chest.

'All right,' says my mother. 'Take what you've got with you. Don't just leave it lying around.'

So we go downstairs. Guy carries nothing, Hugh has his bundle, everything folded neatly again, in his arms, and he goes home. My mother goes out to the kitchen, with the real-estate section of the paper. Guy follows her, to put on the kettle. John plumps himself onto the couch in the sitting room. Michael settles beside him, and on the floor in front he spreads out newspaper. He lays the Sam Browne on it. Then he finds a brush and a tin of Kiwi Dark Tan and an old bottle of Brasso and a rag. John turns on the television. Bent over, Michael concentrates on applying his polish and his Brasso. He rubs hard and he shines the belt to a new glory. Then he stands up and buckles it on over his pink and rose Nepalese jumper. On the television they are just playing 'Advance Australia Fair'. We call out to the kitchen that it's starting, and make slight nervous adjustments to our positions. I sit in the armchair beside the boys, holding the hip flask in my left hand and the binoculars in my right, and together we begin to watch the Rugby Test.

Bequeathing

WHEN I COME to write my last will, the one I wish to be remembered by, and not just the provisional and temporising one, it will have to be a document of some style. The will, even now, is an immature literary form. This is surprising, for the formal requirements are minimal and its teasing attractions are many.

It can be as dramatic or as oblique a self-revelation as you wish. For the central thing about a will is that you specify what is important to you. Instead of being forced into the dreary abstractions of a philosophical statement or a conventional credo, you proceed emblematically. You nominate 'my copy of the first edition of *Gulliver's Travels*' or 'my earthenware torso of a woman, a very early and uncatalogued piece by Jan King' or 'my folder of family birth, marriage and death certificates'.

Or you choose, because you are a different sort of person, or because you would like to create what you consider a misleading impression, 'the marital canteen of cutlery' or 'the round rosewood dining table'. Such nominations I would tend to rate boring, but everything depends on the context. This cataloguing of bourgeois effects and what is apparently utterly material may well represent a final effort to wriggle free from a pinned down transparency. The bohemian or feckless or unencumbered insect is flinging sand up into the downcast eyes of his readers. 'Look what I've been saving up to throw at you,' he laughs. These items he showed no interest in, seemed unaware of, are enumerated, and assigned. Has he been treasuring them all along? Has he been somehow ashamed of his attachments, and freed at last only in this document to be his unreconstructed self? Or is it a last, contemptuous spitting out of the distasteful?

Or you might hover over the blank document, and sentiment might bring to mind any number of trivial, haphazard objects. 'The bone-handled grapefruit knife I have used every morning for the last forty years,' you might find yourself writing, and you lay out just that item as an essay in itself on orderly habits or the clean, sharp palate.

There is nothing to stop the document being comprehensively long. After all here is what you have conserved of, and through, a lifetime. If something is considered precious, it will be best preserved by being named. No point in spending a life engendering, fostering, nourishing something if it can go as easily as you go. Name what is dear to you, give the procession time and room to display itself. Drum up whatever has been a blessing. A will is too easily treated as a document for the future, when it is primarily a stocktake of one's past, a careful specification of the baggage that has been gathered and retained and must now be set in transit. Hence logic demands completeness.

So too of course does the law. It is one of the nicer and more challenging, if not wholly rational, aspects of this genre that a will cannot work unless it is utterly comprehensive. Specify the totality of your property, or the whole thing is worthless. This logical entailment is nothing new: the will, in its best-realised form, is a variety of confession. I have been well drilled in the notion that no matter how apparently fulsome or spectacular a confession may sound, it is – unless I own up to absolutely everything – simply invalid. And a travesty. And a sacrilege. The psychological dangers are the same for both testators and penitents. Such a legal paradigm exacerbates the problems of the timorous soul. You get excessive scrupulosity, a surfeit of self-accusation (just to be on the safe side), and an inattention to one's individual personality.

Nothing has been done to obviate these dangers. Otherwise bold personalities slip quietly into the most formalistic harness. The invitation to declare all is certainly compelling, but it acts as a caution on testators rather than as a challenge to them. They will accept the given phrase rather than run the minimal risk of an omission which will invalidate their preferred distribution.

'All my furniture plate plated goods linen glass china books (except books of account) pictures prints statuary musical instruments clothing jewellery ...' my father writes to us. It is highly unlikely that he owns any linen or china or prints. He most certainly does not own any books of account, statuary, musical instruments, or any personal ornament that could be dignified with the title of jewellery. The trouble is his immovable respect for the professional. He presumes that any lawyer he deals with, just as surely as any doctor in another branch of medicine he deals with, is technically competent to the point of being one of the best in his line of work. He is quite wrong. The archaic formula, archaic even by legal standards, would be a red light to any opinion even marginally more informed than his own.

Still, his misguided trust is not so much the point as his failure to seize the chance to lay his finger on a lifetime's personal effects. In his case his decision is eloquently the correct one: whereof one cannot speak, thereof one lets another do the talking. 'Possessions' is a foreign word to him. There is no object that his hand has ever lingered on. There is nothing he has ever ambitioned for, much less lusted after. He has passed through the world and what he has accumulated is merely, he imagines, the entailment of a life of dedication. If that entailment isn't there, either the dedication itself, or the worthwhileness of its object, is suspect. But he has never examined closely or turned back to fondle anything that came to the surface in his wake. Like a good son of the gospels he has kept his hand to the plough, and looked ahead and treasured the same things that he has always treasured and that belong to no one: the success of pupils, the Sydney coastline, the panache of sportsmen and the frisson of their competition, phrases from the more cobwebby interstices of literature, the lighter side of colleagues, and his wife. Such objects are not specified in wills.

This insouciance about the impedimenta of life has, like all virtues, its disruptive side. For the will of course not only specifies what is cherished, but also who is cherished, and it conjoins them. But if the testator is not attached to anything much, he can still be subject to the tugs of benevolence and solicitude, and yet he is without any personalised and emblematic way of displaying that largeness of heart. In a floundering way he senses needs and obligations and feels the rush of blood, but has nothing in his hands that is quite appropriate, and so, like any caricature of the constrained philanthropist, he digs in and shoves out a fistful of money. The effect is as untidy as the gesture itself.

That is not quite to do justice to the subtlety of some financial bequests. My grandfather, commercially several stages further evolved than his eldest son, deployed his bequests with a rich plenitude of meaning. There was money, a four-figure sum but hardly more, to fund an annual lecture that would have his name attached. Two offerings were made, one to each of the British and the Australian Colleges of Surgeons, not so much that it made any significant difference to his estate, but neither so little that the bequests could be declined. Equally, enough to make it plausible that these were contributions to the expansion and communication of surgical knowledge but also enough to fuel an argument that they were essentially a gesture of vanity. Why otherwise tie the beneficiaries down to a lecture with his name attached? Oh, he had his detractors, my grandfather, and this was one of their sturdier-seeming arguments. What can I say? He had the right to specify. After all, autocratic, unquestionable specification is the great right of the testator, probably more so than at any other time in life. And who would want to delimit a naturally bold personality as he takes this stage for the one and only time. A donation to petty cash or general revenue would be a diffuse, anaemic gesture, and no incentive to good housekeeping either.

Why did he have to put his name to it? Well, the lecture had to be given some name. If it were to be called after some as yet unhonoured, and therefore probably minor, hero of medicine, the preliminaries of explanation would constitute a longeur. It would have to include a reference to the benefactor. Why not simply title it with the benefactor's name and be done with it? Because, say my grandfather's detractors, it is not acceptable procedure for a man to nominate himself. Becoming modesty suggests that's the job of a widow, child, friend. Besides, he's trying to get his own name up in lights, but gets away with being pettily mean about it.

There's hysteria in this, and the first trace of an ill-will towards the old man that I can't allow. Such is the combustible nature of wills. The loves, duties and debts of a testator, in all their gradings, are never reproducible. People scan wills with a more instinctual malevolence than they accord any other literary document. It is all grist to my demand that a will should be a careful, individual construction. Not to ward off the malice that might otherwise be shown it. There is no deflecting those bent on ill-will. Accept that you're going to be vilified, or at least muttered about, that there is no standardising tastes or human partialities, that those whom you love might only erratically love one another – first you must accept that and a host of the other minutiae that make up human chaos. Then you sketch this one-off image of a never-to-be-repeated incarnation that is yourself, using as your medium to describe it only an apposition between the material baggage and the loves you have accumulated. Whatever the detractors might wish, their rancour about allocations can only cringe shamefully and irrelevantly in front of this consummated, inviolable personality.

Yet the document might achieve this emblematic status quite by misadventure. In my father's case it was his misguided sense of duty that led to his leaving a messy and largely ineffectual will. Exactly as it should have been for a man of his unworldliness. At first he saw no need to add any personal mark to the formula handed him, a document already rich in personality in its characterlessness. But when he was given an approximate, give or take a year or two, date for his death, he began to fret that the formula might be callously indifferent to moral shadings. He had three granddaughters – 'fatherless children'. Their father was in fact unproblematically alive, merely divorced from their mother, but in constant generous contact with his daughters.

'Those fatherless little girls,' says my father, his tears straining at their ducts.

'Well, they're not, technically. Nor in fact,' says whoever he has for company.

My father looks reproachful, even scathing. His blood still heats up under this moral slackness, this mincing of words, and maybe even this self-interest.

The company retreats. If you're sensitive to reputation, and to wrong words in the wrong place that will go down in your history, you don't argue with a man about the drawing up of his will. It is another of the privileges of the genre.

'There's not much else I can do for them.' He grieves that he is so limited, but there is also visible a frustrated indignation that things have been allowed to reach this pass, that he is having to salvage what wouldn't have been endangered if his own principles had been observed. The annoyance hovers threateningly over anyone who happens to be his company. They have been stained by the same non-compliance, and the admonition is general. He is calm about death, my father, but not about the intractability of the living.

'You can't reason with him', says my mother. 'Don't think you're the only one that's tried to speak to him. If Michael can't get through to him ...' She puts out her hand for the tea caddy. 'Would you get me out the cake tin?' she says.

'You think he would at least take a lesson out of his own father's book.'

'Well I wouldn't say this publicly, but I really do think he believes he was superior to his father in some ways.'

She is thinking of pious bequests. My father's uprightness, religious observance and respect for the clergy cannot be rated second to anyone's. But he pays his homage to the institution of the church, and to its individual representatives, not to any proliferation of pious bodies. He sees his religion as more advanced and more masculine than his father's. The old man makes bequests to the religious orders he had more time for or time with: $200 each to the Christian Brothers, the Sisters of Mercy, the Redemptorists. In each case the money entails Masses for the repose of his soul. It should have netted him twenty holy sacrifices from each legatee. It would not occur to my father to take out such insurance. He has enough sense of the Reformation and its ructions to find even this style of spiritual trafficking a little distasteful. The old man was still enough of his mother's son and his wife's clay to list in these provisions without a second thought – if, also, without any desperate urge for eternal self-preservation. He was far more interested in paying respects to bodies who had benefited him than in clamouring for their prayers. His son does not consider a will a place for paying tributes of thanks. Generally he does not have a strong sense of indebtedness. That is not to say he is not conscious of help given and does not acknowledge this on occasion. Without any display of detachment or natural severity of manner he is not a man who betrays reliance.

He has disciplined himself to avoid the overt betrayals of need and desire. He hardly ever touches, even glancingly or in play. He allows himself to be kissed, by those whose kisses he does not need. But he is without irony, and not needing their kisses means simply that; he takes them gratefully but they are not a breath that he requires in order to live. Of course a kiss – certainly a peck, even if lingering – draws in far more breath than it exhales. The lips land and their muscles contract just slightly, and the pop initiates the sucking movement. Their kisses are the pilgrim's stretching out to draw power from the dying saint. Part of him knows that this tribute is being paid. With the detached air of the holy man he does not cling, or he does not think he clings, to anyone.

'Let's get this settled,' says my father. It is a matter of equity not affections. The lawyer comes. The lawyer is incompetent and illiterate. My father is having a preliminary encounter with death. He requests an additional clause about his fatherless grand-daughters. The lawyer ends up with fives divided by three rather than five multiplied by three. He is also innumerate. But by now my father has a grandson, and in his fever and his pain he glimpses a lurching inequity in these steps he is taking. So he adds another paragraph and apportions to his grandson. As the lawyer fumbles, my father makes a bid to tidy it up by designating that the grandson must share his portion with any sibling *in utero* at the time of his grandfather's death.

'What about the not-yet-conceived? Why should they be discriminated against?'

'I can't worry about them.'

'You shouldn't be worrying about any grandchildren. But if you're going to, you should at least follow the logic of it.'

'What I've done, I've done.'

'It's the very ones you've never seen or who have never known you at all that could most do with some sort of gesture from you.'

'Oh, it won't worry them.'

'It's your business and your decision. But I've got to say, and then I'll shut up, that this sort of … thing is what creates trouble for families.'

Maybe my mother says that. Maybe it is not her.

After lunch, on the day after her father-in-law's funeral, my mother, quite unannounced, took the floor, the first time she had ever done so. She wouldn't do it again for ten years, not until her husband were dead. The tears were lurking, but they went no further. She neither started because of a rush of emotion, nor did she break down as she went on.

'He was the centre of things for us all. A lot of the reason for us coming together. Now that he's gone, the thing he would want most of all is that we should stay united and friendly and in touch with one another all the time. He was very proud of his family, all of his family. The family is everything. Other friends come and go, but please God we'll always be able to rely on our family, always have them.'

The old man in fact had been selective about family. His younger grandchildren he never tried to distinguish. His children-in-law he tended to think of as intruders and not quite up to scratch. He was gallant to them, and generous, but he did not keep his reservations to himself. His children-in-law knew this, and lived with it, lightly. My mother had stood up to the old man, come to like him, and decided that what he stood for was good. Looking around with scepticism and despair, she falls back on the family.

Her husband's will is a family document. Her father-in-law's had another, a tribal dimension. Her husband mentions only wife and grandchildren and the one child who at the time of writing is married and has children. It is merely the way it works out, but the divorced and the childless are not named. He has written what he has written and he lives, and when another grandson comes he is tired of it all and he abandons the processes of the law. He hands me a letter as I am boarding a plane, for merely a fortnight out of the country, and has inscribed the envelope 'to be opened in flight'.

Once before he has done a similar thing. Thirteen years previously I am going overseas for the first time, going to Ireland, and in the envelope is a cheque for $200 with a note attached, which reads simply 'to take yourself to Europe, and not to be spent on women'. Never forget a sense of humour, even a father's, but the joke has an edge. I have never heard of him making a similar remark to any of my brothers. He is firing a light-hearted warning shot on behalf of the family. There is one danger to the family – and the notion may be unoriginal and murkily masculine, but for all that it has a durability and a mythic status that leaves it far from contemptible – and that danger is 'other women' or, in the bachelor's case, a strongly developed pre-marital taste for them. It's the waywardness, the centrifugality of the urge. You're part of the family centre yourself, and so the whole kit and caboodle is supposed to fall apart. The family cannot hold.

As it happens I am an emissary for the family. My father has got his name in the papers, in the international papers too, and Maureen Cavanagh in the republican village of Coalisland in County Tyrone is lining her kitchen cupboards, and there on the floor is a doctor with the same rare surname as her mother's maiden name and a birthplace in this very county (wrong), and he has made good in Australia. These are bad times in the North, writes Maureen, and I thought that if I could get some assistance I might come out and join the family in Australia. It'll be high summer out here soon, the family writes back, not a good time for a person from the North to land in Australia. But our eldest son will be over there soon, and he'd love to get in touch with you, hear all about the family and fill you in.

Not on women, says my father. Maureen is girlish, nervous with excitement, lets on that she has a new dress, has had her hair permed and coloured, and is entirely at my disposal. I probably do not spend one penny on her the whole of my 48 hour visit. But at our second meal together she tells me she has cancer, and that she needs to go to Australia for a cure. At the end of lunch in the Royal Hotel, Omagh, when Maureen goes to the Ladies, her husband, Joe, tells me this is all imagination. She is perfectly well, as it were. Joe shows no interest in salvation in Australia. He conducts me around the sights of the locality, various ruins and bomb sites, and clicks his tongue half-heartedly. Maureen takes the back seat while he tells me a tale of tribal loyalty. One night he notices a lot of military activity on the road outside. He knows there are a couple of old fellows, veterans of the War of Independence, up from the Free State. They're having a meeting with a certain lot of younger fellows. He puts the german shepherd on the chain, goes out for an evening stroll through the troops and the jeeps and the lorries, up to the house where they're all at, and just mentions what's going on around the corner. 'Terrible times,' says Joe, 'awful business all this bombing.'

'We'd be better away from it all,' says Maureen.

'We can thank God we've moved on from all that,' says my father later. 'One doesn't have to be a snob, or disown them, but we can acknowledge we've come on from there, and be grateful for it.' He's been nowhere near the place, had nothing to do with the country since 1947, the last straw being an unemptied chamber-pot under the guest bed in his mother's childhood home.

'Not that it isn't a wonderful country, and our home,' says Maureen.

'There is a thing called progress.' My father is stirred. 'There's no point in denying it. Of course you'll only manage it if you're prepared for a little bit of work and a lot of discipline. People don't like discipline. That's where the trouble is.'

'Did you think,' asks Maureen,'that where the family came from would be like this?'

'We can only be grateful,' my father shakes his head, 'that the old man made the break, when he did. I won't deny they have a great number of qualities, and we've a lot to be grateful to them for. But. Some things are best left behind.'

My father's grandfather began the climb. From being a labourer in the Glasgow shipyards, dependent on his wife's dressmaking while he went through his veterinary science. My father is happy that I should inspect the source. So I look for the grave of the old vet, my great grandfather. He had died in the house of his brother, a tailor, Maureen's own grandfather.

Joe smokes in the car while I peruse the parish registers. The surname is there. But the only entry is for William, the tailor. It's in the baptismal register. Maureen in her fur hovers at my shoulder, demure and awkward in a sacristy. The priest sits behind me, not interfering, seeing I have a grasp of the method of the book. The index shows that William has had seven children baptised. The mother is also named in each case. William, my great grandfather's brother, has had three different mothers for his children. Only one of the women bears his surname. It might be the variant habits of whichever priest made each entry. But in brackets after the name of one of the infants is the annotation 'illeg'. I don't crane forward, but I look at it carefully to see if it might not mean 'illegible'. But I can't find any plausibility for that reading. I turn to the priest. 'Does that mean what I presume it means?'

He has clearly registered the annotation himself. 'I believe it must,' he says. His voice has just the smallest, correct degree of embarrassment, and of apology, and of amusement. There is no trace of anger.

Maureen peers over. I have no idea how well she reads. I say nothing. I get out my pen and notebook and start to take the entry down. I transfer the father and the women and the babies. I come to the child marked 'illeg' and its mother, Letitia Devlin, and I write down the date of its birth, and I see that it was born five and half months after another child of this same William, but this time by his wife. I stare, unseeing now, at the paper, and I begin to moon about all the possibilities in that story.

'Let's put it this way,' says my father. 'Certain things are better left behind. Any decent hard-working person would prefer not to know about them. And that's how it ought to be.'

My father's belief is an inherited notion, though subtlety and an epigrammatic boldness have been lost in transition. His own father has a summary view of marriages. He sees fellows with proclivities and despicable traits beyond tolerance, and he can find only one reason why a woman would stand it. 'A woman will forgive a fulla anything - meanness, the lot - if he doesn't look at other women.'

A remark like this can have a tone of clinical observation, that yet betrays an almost amused disbelief at the irrational imbalance of the equation. Or it can be the spat-out self-pitying of the aggrieved man, confident in his possession of all the necessary virtues but stung by a woman's holding against him a minor self-indulgence. I hear no trace of this second tone in my grandfather's remark. Sexuality interests him, but as an object of professional observation. My grandfather's wife had probably no interest of any sort in it for the last thirty years of her life, but I can't spot even a perfidious tinge to the countless references he makes to her.

Can sexual habits be presumed to run in the family? They can of course be encouraged to do so, and wills have a unsettling tradition of being repositories for sermons and sanctions on this score. 'In the event of my widow remarrying ...' might be primarily an economic stipulation so that a testator's goods pass duly to his own begotten, but there are flickers of jealousy too around the edges of the prescription, of an embargo on any further sexual activity. My father's will does not omit this common provision. But it is the will, in its autonomy, that includes it. He goes along with it, he could not imagine her remarriage because he could not bear it. But he cannot bring himself to say so, not in words of his own. He accepts the formula, and puts his name to it, and it does reflect his wishes, but the words are alien. They are such a remote, legal set of sentences that they have an air of being both inevitable and universal. To date he has got what he wanted, but bears no responsibility for making any personal gesture towards it. The will accommodates him.

When it doesn't ... I open his envelope once the seat belt sign has been turned off. Without preamble or advertence to the maze that has led to this odd outlet, he informs me that he is transferring to me a parcel of shares to be held in trust, for the child I have and any future children I have by Louella, my wife. And only by her.

This sting, of course, allows no distinction between, on the one hand, children of a later, post-divorce, marriage or, naturally, children of no marriage at all and, on the other, the children of any later, post-bereavement, marriage. Perhaps this final possibility doesn't occur to him. Perhaps it does, but he considers the probabilities are against it, or at least that to make allowance for it would disturb the straightforward lines of his instruction. He has a point to make and he will not cloud it with some exception. In any case it is in keeping with his ideal of fidelity to one partner, no matter what the circumstances. If he demand it of a wife, equally he should demand it of a child. Besides, it is the thinking of a tough, and central, theological tradition: the widow who is truly a widow retires to the life of celibacy on the death of the spouse. Virginity is, as it were, regained. In his copy of *Religo Medici* my father has underscored the words 'This trivial and vulgar way of union, it is the foolishest act a wise man commits in all his life'. It is not that dreariest cliché of all – the Irish-Catholic sexual hang-up. Sir Thomas Browne represents a profounder and more universal disquiet than that. My father has a chance to corral that absurdity. Or at least he believes he sees a tendency for it to run wild, and he tries to hold it back with ... a whip or is it a carrot? Something of both.

The communication is eerie and it has its amusing side. But it hurts. There would be the one obvious victim, but my father has already made it clear that any grandchild he has not known he is not interested in. It is a short step from there to positive rejection, to the wilderness of Nod. The sins of the father shall be visited on the child. In fact the father shall go scot free – apart from the humiliation of the parental finger shaking from the grave. Yet this conditional gift is not part of his will. He has thrown me a curly moral one to juggle. He does not include it in his will. His admonition is private, as is his benefaction. He does not give his instruction the compelling force of law. He kicks and caresses at the same time. He mistrusts, and then again he wholly trusts that the very object of his mistrust will enact the penalty against himself. My father goes to his grave an ingenu – but an ingenu with moments of psychological deftness. He allows freedom so that the honour done to him may be all the greater when his children do his will and observe all his wishes from a state of freedom rather than as predestined slaves. Thy will be done.

The will turns out to be but a wish after all. Not enforceable, legally or any other way. My father's will is examined and it is discovered that his second thoughts have not been thought through. He and his innumerate solicitor have forgotten to forage for the funds he has allotted to his fatherless granddaughters and the grandson who bolted in before the customary way of law became too great a problem. There is nothing for them. His will effects nothing that would not have been done had he died intestate.

The family foundations rock very gently. There is not a great deal of debris. My mother positions herself under it, sweeping here and there. Some of this should not be lost or is reusable. She has an eye for what is no use to her but would be of benefit somewhere else. 'What good would that be to me in the new place?' she asks. 'I can't take very much there.'

She allocates pictures hanging from the wall. 'You've always liked that,' she says to me. 'You should have it.' It's entitled *Richmond Cemetery*. The viewer stands on a track that leads into the fenced-off area where the gravestones are barely visible above the vegetation. Beyond is the sea and sky. The scene is dry, linear, and quite without a romantic quality. This place of the dead is unrecognisable. No Richmond that I know is by the sea. It is impossible nowadays to know what you are getting with a Richmond. A pleasure park? A struggletown? Merely a stop on the journey into the central desert? To look on this scene there is no telling who the company are, whether the sea is an eternal solace or whether its presence is a trick of perspective or in fact a complete licence on the part of the artist. Does the dry bleakness give way to other seasons? Is the homely unpretentiousness of it a comfort - or an abandonment of any attempt to ennoble the scene? The painting says nothing definite about the dead. I'd have preferred, say, Waverley, where the serried dead, in due proportions of the celebrated and the obscure, are forever tumbling towards the Pacific, and the ocean, set between its playful havens of Clovelly and Bronte, is at its most benign. The urns and the angels and the putti and the crosses, even in their brokenness, flash back in chorus with the dance of the sun and shadow and white flecks on the ocean below. But Richmond Cemetery is not that, and it is what I am being given. 'You'd better get it valued,' says my mother.

The dealer says, 'It's a good one of his, and a nice-sized canvas, and fairly early. If the subject were terrace houses, I'd put 55 on it. He's appreciated a lot just recently.' He hardly needs to say more, but he does. 'But it's not terrace houses. In fact you'd have to say that the subject has a limited market. Not everyone would have ... that on their drawing-room walls. Even less their office. If I had it in the gallery I'd mark it down to 35 and try and turn it over quickly. But for purposes of insurance, well, say 15.'

I remove some framed family photographs from the wall on the landing and put *Richmond Cemetery* there. I pass it every time I go into the bedroom or the bathroom. The landing is narrow and the light there has gone, so that it is impossible to get a perspective on the painting or even a clear, illuminated view of it. But it is out of the sun, it is not ostentatious, it need not upset or distract the more casual visitor who does not get past the public rooms. In fact the cemetery hardly sees the light of day.

So my mother has second thoughts. 'If you're not going to display it ... ' she says. 'It's yours, certainly. You're the only one who's ever shown any interest in it. But I feel I should hang onto it for the moment. It will go to you. It's yours already. But I just don't feel it's right, in view of everything, that you should be the one with it at the moment. I think it should stay with me for the present. But it's yours, and it goes to you when I die.'

Botany
Cemetery

Incongruities are rife. There is precious little rest for the spirit here.

(i)

Beside the encrusted Italianate wall stands a white Gemini. The front passenger door is open. In the seat reclines a woman in her late thirties. She reads, or at least she has on her lap, a copy of *New Idea*. But she glances up, still with an expression of radical boredom, at any external movement – another vehicle, an adjusted hose, a bird. She sees, she does not register, she is unmoved. Between her open door and an elaborate vault is a man, a little older than herself. He kneels on one knee, and on the other thigh he rests his elbow and leans his forehead into the palm of his hand. In his free right hand he holds a rosary, and with it he makes the sign of the cross, and seems to strap himself. His head slides up and down the slipway of his hand, and he wails at the grim medallion of an old tight-bunned woman on the vault. Inside the car his wife uses *New Idea* as a fan.

(ii)

Only here, in all this city, are there no machines used. The metal bites and slices and opens up the cavity according to the pressure of palm and wrist and shoulder, and heel. The diggers stand in the messy beginnings of the wound, lay down the tough angular clamp, and brace it back against the earth. Then they go on down, in.

The paling ribs are inserted and tapped in, and the exoskeleton takes shape. Its internal organs pulse away rhythmically. They scour and dislodge and remove. They tone up here, strengthen there, they redistribute pressure, they break up the solids, they eject what is extraneous. They murmur as they work. Just once or twice they falter or stutter in their rhythm. The longer they work, the more detritus they accumulate and the more subdued and unreliable becomes the beat of their activity. It is a fast-growing but short life this creature has. It is rare, seldom noticed, perfect in it purpose, and does not draw out its end. Now its organs desist. Just the shell remains. The empty thing is ready.

The blunt-headed, tapering outline is pleasing. Most like a crocodile in its shape, it promises bland unaimiability, surprising speed in attack, strong jaws, and the capacity for rapid disposal. Or, like a child's toy, its aperture beckons for the mirror image shape to pass through. The intelligent child works it from both sides. The shape that was made for it rises up and comes out again as easily as it went in.

This is an insertion exercise. The earth is being prepared for the intrusion of a foreign body. It is staked down and forcibly opened. It is not patently diseased, but then it is not yet really anything. It needs the admixture of another, more complex, element. So an injection is prepared. The new unpredictable compound of chemical and memorialised human quirks is implanted. No one can quantify the effects. But the implant represents a gamble: lodged and sewn in there in the hope that there might be produced a new earth. It is a gamble worth running with. That perhaps eventually the ground might quake, the hills might leap like young lambs, the mountains like calves, the cages of the earth burst open, and, of all things, the dead be everywhere and making their appearances to many.

(iii)

He is visited, but he is never allowed complete attention. Sick and dying he was the only figure of interest. But the circumstances of death give a later, and final, twist to the perspective. He is on the western end of his short row. At the eastern end is the daughter of an old friend of his wife's. She has reached here four months before him. She is just thirty-four. She has been murdered. No bond of fellowship between the surgeon and the young woman forces itself on the visitor. This woman is sacred ground. You tread lightly and warily and you do no flippant violence to her. She has earned inviolability. My mother tends the one grave, with its common-place, almost painless inscription. But her sharing in her own communion of saints takes her every time to say hello, as she calls it, to Carolyn.

My mother does her stations at the graves. It is restrained religion. She is straightforward and severely practical. She snips the grass, she brushes weed and dreck and the build-up of sand. Then she stands back and leaves a decade of the rosary or perhaps three Hail Marys. Never a gratuitous number. Never some unrehearsed aspirations. She has to leave a message that is recognisable. She communicates through the formulas and formalities. Her husband will register that it is her this way. And it is the only approach to a young woman whom she may have met as a child, and to whom no personal words of consolation are possible. So she passes from west to east, from the bent, haggard, consumed shell to the suddenly shattered vessel of energy. Along my mother's beat a thin but sturdy mat of couch grass is growing over the sandy grey soil. It is all her husband wants; any efflorescence would be otiose. There is achievement here already; no one disputes that. These are near enough to old bones, and nothing more is expected of them. They moulder quietly, and the old waves of virtue go out of them. The spirit is stable and satisfied, and no breakouts are looked for or even needed. But to the east, on the grave of the murdered woman, there is the oddest emblem of defiance against arrested life. This grave, this grave alone, is carpeted with horse manure.

(iv)

The lawn is on a slope of perhaps one in five. Across the bottom runs a narrow gulley. On the other side is a similar slope, and the two slopes arch around amphitheatrically to the west, and are hitched together there by the belt of the vaults of the Italians. On the farther slope are the white statuary and angular proclamations of the Greeks. They shimmer towards the north-east. You shade your eyes against them to the south-east, and the gulley runs away from you towards, of all things, a market garden. There, along the raised beds edging forward through the lush greenery of shallots, spring onions, chinese cabbages, leeks, beetroot – all the plenty of the force-fed bulbs – are the coolie hats. Here, where there should only be sand and desolation, they move imperceptibly inland along the lines of their fruitfulness. Then they turn and ease themselves back again while the smudged water in the Landing Place at Phillip Bay laps at their heels and toes. You can see the waves bringing and the waves taking, in and out along the gully into this place. This is the Vale of Jehosaphat. Where the nations are gathered.

The horizon refuses to stabilise. When you lie on the slope of this shallow bowl, the horizon will not withdraw its distance. The rim becomes the horizon. The world loses its infinite seductive possibilities. It is of merely a child's circumference. All its elements are visible and operable at once.

The horizon is out of keeping. By the standards of eternal rest. It is jagged metal. The great energy of Bunnerong power station has left this vast one-off fossil. The black, rust-smudged, silver-streaked steel looms over the vaults and the Greeks and the sandy lawn. Chimneys, pipes, conduits, pressure caps, springs, runnels, guy-lines, stacks – a general exaltation of metal in which all configurations and sizes are rising. But it is silent, it is dead. Besides, the flourishes of cast steel give only a tiny minority their cultural uplift. How many enlightened patrons of a late-twentieth-century aesthetic do you see lazing here? This place is not fashionable. Those that come to lie here have never been enlightened. Those more likely to claim appreciativeness succumb in the end to roses and ash and a plot of earth made sweet by their own romantic dispensation. But this horizon here is striated metal.

I say, it has its appositeness. He is used to the final mercy emerging from the abrupt edges of sharp metal. He is adamant that hope lies only in a detached, cold, steely concentration. He has an ineradicable yearning for the comfort of tears, the rising note, and the velleities and prayers of soft flesh. But it has never been enough, and however fiercely he regrets it, he knows that warm roseate goodwill can never have the effect of the remote gloved hand leaning over the metal.

He sinks back and rests in the carefully disposed suitability of his situation. But between one viewing and the next, the metal is razed. The scrap merchants lumber away with the junk. Now the horizon is flat, bare, utterly without character. He takes it in. So this is not final.